D1059862

TRUE AND UNTRUE
AND OTHER NORSE TALES

TRUE AND UNTRUE
AND OTHER NORSE TALES

Edited and compiled by
SIGRID UNDSET

* * *

Illustrated by Frederick T. Chapman

CLUNY
Providence, Rhode Island

CLUNY MEDIA EDITION, 2023

This Cluny edition is a republication of the 1962 edition
of *True and Untrue and Other Norse Tales*,
first published in 1945 by Alfred A. Knopf.

These tales are based on the original stories collected by Moe and Asbjørnsen.

For information regarding this title
or any other Cluny Media publication,
please write to info@clunymedia.com, or to
Cluny Media, P.O. Box 1664, Providence, RI 02901

* VISIT US ONLINE AT WWW.CLUNYMEDIA.COM *

Cluny edition copyright © 2023 Cluny Media LLC

All rights reserved.

ISBN (PAPERBACK) | 978-1685951993
ISBN (HARDCOVER) | 978-1685952020

Cover design by Clarke & Clarke
Cover image: Theodor Kittelsen, *Far, Far Away Soria Moria Palace
Shimmered Like Gold*, 1900, oil on canvas
Courtesy of Wikimedia Commons

CONTENTS

FOREWORD: THE ADVENTURE STORY OF THE FOLK TALE

* * *

I

IF you like folk tales and if you have read the folk tales of different nations, you will have noticed the family likeness among a number of stories from countries separated by thousands of miles of land and ocean. You may have wondered how it could happen, that much the same kind of tales should be told in almost every corner of the globe. Is it because all men are brothers under the skin, and the things that matter the most to all of us are in the end very much the same, so that when we invent stories about the world as we know it, or as we would like it to be, we unconsciously invent almost the same stories? Or is it because the tales have wandered?

The answer to both of these questions is yes. Everywhere in the world parents love their children; boys and girls have wanted to marry someone they liked better than anyone else; and everywhere most young people would not mind if the beloved one could also contribute something to their future prosperity—say half a kingdom, or the giant's hoard of gold, or just a fine farm or a snug little cottage. All over the world man has felt attached to the beach where he had his cottage and his boat, or to the fields he tilled, or to his native land. And everywhere the people knew, that when one man was loyal to his tribe or his country, it meant protection to all of them, and that he would defend his home soil with courage and cunning. But they also saw how important it was to have wise men among them—lawgivers, inventors of improved weapons and implements and of better ways to utilize the resources of their environment. And so all tribes, and all nations, have told tales and made songs about their heroes—the warriors as well as the heroes who revealed to them spiritual truths and new ways to increase in material culture. Most men have felt sure that generosity, kindness, a sense of justice, and sincerity are good things. But most men also admire a clever trickster, at least as long as he does not play his tricks at their expense. Most men delight in wit, astuteness and practical jokes. Because so much of the subject matter of folk tales is common human nature, there are good reasons to believe that similar stories have been invented by different people, at different times. When wandering tribes met and mixed, peacefully or by conquest, they would learn each other's tales, and then old stories might be changed because a similar story of some other tribe seemed more beautiful or witty. And sometimes people learned a story that was quite new to them.

For the tales have also wandered. Students of folklore have tried to trace some basic types of folk tales across continents and back through the ages, as far as records can be found. And scholars have advanced a number of theories about the origin and the wanderings of this ancient lore. Most of these theories cannot be definitely proved, nor can they be disproved. Here is one about the origin of the story of "Little Red Riding Hood."

A school of anthropologists that flourished in Vienna before World War II supposed—and they gathered material which partly proves they were on the right track—that when man first appeared on earth, small groups of men and women roaming wide in search of their livelihood, got separated and came to live so far apart that their descendants did not meet for many thousands of years. Each in their isolated area of settlement evolved entirely different ways of life. The Viennese school spoke of *Kulturkreise*, meaning spheres of culture. This was when the great glacier still covered most of Europe, North America down beyond the Great Lakes, and Asia, all the way into the middle of present-day China. Sometimes the icecap would recede for ages, sometimes it advanced. Then men and animals alike who lived near the edge of the glacier had to move south.

Farthest to the south, probably along the great rivers of India and Burma, little bands, armed with sticks and heavy stones which they carried in their fists, clubbed a path through the jungle. On small clearings they erected their flimsy shelters of poles and palm fronds and plaited grass. Although they later developed cudgels from the sticks, and from the fist-stones, maces and axes, in the beginning they were so severely handicapped against the wild animals of the jungle that they lived mostly on shellfish and fish from the rivers, and on the vegetable food they could gather—roots, fruit and seeds. In those early days women were just as efficient as men when it came to providing food for the household. And then, maybe because she had noticed that when seeds had been spilled in the dumps of dirt and offal by the shelters, the edible plants grew lush and large, some wise woman scratched the ground around her hut and put in some seeds on purpose, before she dropped the garbage on it (for cleanliness was still an undiscovered pleasure—the people just left their filth all around the place). So the first garden in the world was started. That women first cultivated vegetables, and that the beginning of agriculture was gardening, seem tolerably certain. Since in this type of culture woman became the chief provider and food producer, a way of life developed which has been called matriarchy.

The head of the family was the mother. Her children stayed with her all their lives. They made friends with the sons and daughters of other mothers, but we would not call the relation between the young people of different families marriages, since the couples never moved away from their mothers to set up homes of their own. (In the end, of course, marriage was introduced, or re-introduced, because many young people wanted to move out and clear a place of their own and be together always—and I suppose they wanted to get away from the almighty matriarchs!) But for ages the daughters and granddaughters, with their children, lived with the old mother, and the sons had neither rights nor duties towards their children in another mother's household, but educated their sisters' sons in the crafts and the duties of the tribesmen.

Now I have read how someone of the Viennese school suggested that the first Little Red Riding Hood was not a sweet little girl, but a naughty boy who wanted more than his share, or his ration, of the food his grandmother raised in her garden. He broke into the family plot at night and rifled the vegetable beds. And the original Red Hood was his own raw and bloody pate, because when Grandmother discovered his wickedness she had him scalped. The bad boy survived, but he did not mend his ways. So in the end came the big bad wolf—and inside the wolf was Grandmamma. Though it was not because the wolf had swallowed her. She came in her ceremonial robes of animal hides that she used when she made magic to protect her garden. She killed the bad boy, and his relatives ate him at a sacrificial meal. However, whether this is the original story about Red Riding Hood or not, I would not venture to say.

In the north of Asia, near the edge of the great glacier, were tundras and marshes and shallow lakes, fed by the waters from the icecap. The marshes and the lakes teemed with bird life; and the tundras and the grassy plains farther south were alive with herds of grass-eaters—deer, antelopes, wild cattle and horses. Even primitive men could sometimes trap these in holes dug into the ground and covered with branches; or they might kill a deer by throwing stones and sticks, or by slingshots. They lived on the meat and dressed in the hides, for this was a cold country. From the hides they also made portable shelters—tents—when they had to be on the move following after the trekking herds. In the end these first hunters invented the spear and the javelin, by tipping their sticks with bone and splinters of flint; they also constructed bows and arrows. The men, stronger and more agile, unhampered by the care and carrying of children, became the chief providers. The culture of the tribe was now patriarchal for the father was the head of the family, and his sons stayed with him. But he let them bring home their wives and he married his daughters to the sons of other men. Because the men were more important, he wanted the sons of his sons to belong to his own hunting party.

At some time in these distant ages, it occurred to the hunters to cut off some of the animals from the herds and drive them into a pocket in the hills, from which they could not easily escape, these animals to be held as a meat reserve. The men proceeded to build artificial corrals for their trapped reindeer or cattle. By accident, and by using their powers of observation and deduction, they discovered that some kinds of animals will thrive and breed in captivity, and that some of them would even become quite tame. (Maybe this was the children's contribution to civilization, as the herdboys played with the young animals and made pets of them.) Man had begun the domestication of animals and came to see that tamed animals could be put to many uses, besides being used as meat. The primitive hunters became nomads, moving over the steppes with their herds of reindeer or cattle and horses, learning to know the stars and how to take their bearings from them. The men who owned the largest herds were wealthy men—the first on the face of the earth. The wealthiest became the lords of their tribes, and when they died they left their riches and their chieftainship to their sons.

For the poor young men the easiest way to better their fortunes was to raid other tribes and carry off their cattle, as well as their children and young women. For with wealth slavery entered the world of men. And with slaves to do the most onerous work of the household, the wives and daughters of the rich men enjoyed leisure and luxury. So wealthy fathers took pride in their daughters, as creatures of a nobler breed, superior to the women of the common people, and particularly to the bondwomen of alien stock. A young man who wanted to win a girl of his own tribe for his wife had to prove his mettle by deeds of daring and cunning; he had to get hold of cattle or other treasure for his prospective father-in-law. Especially the precious daughters of a chieftain had to be bought at a great price.

Now the theory is that the folk tales of the poor young man, who by courage or by sagacity and quick wits succeeds in winning the King's daughter and half a kingdom, originated in ancient stories about the exploits of young men who wanted to convince a chieftain's family that he might be a valuable addition to their strength if they would accept him as a son-in-law. This theory seems more likely than the one about the origin of the story of Red Riding Hood, for it is a fact that until quite recently, among many nomadic people, a young man had to make a name for himself—usually by horse-stealing or robbery from neighboring tribes—before he could hope to marry a woman of his own people. For all I know it may still be the custom in out-of-the-way places in Asia or Africa.

As the tales were handed down through the ages, among people who had outgrown the nomadic way of life, the tests the boy had to pass to win the King's daughter became more and more fanciful, remote from everyday life. He had to raid the underworld of the trolls, or fetch the treasures of the giants for the King, or guess the answer to weird questions, or find the magic remedies against sinister witchcraft. Or the whole matter was turned into a joke, and a king would promise his sulky daughter to whoever could make her laugh, or his fibbing daughter to the boy who could out-fib her, or his arrogant and pert daughter to the fellow who could make her shut up!

It is pleasant to be told that the women who had been carried off to a faraway country as bondwomen may sometimes have been rescued and brought back in triumph to their own homes by daring raiders. As the sagas of these expeditions of liberation and revenge echoed down the ages, these would be transformed into the tales of princesses, who were saved from giants and ugly trolls with three or six or nine heads, by gallant young adventurers, who might be princes in their own right, or sons of poor cottagers who proved that they were fit to be kings, and so won the princess and half the kingdom.

II

THE fact we know for certain is, that a number of the folk tales have a pedigree reaching far back into the dim past. They preserve memories of how the world looked to primitive man.

Now there is no reason to believe that primitive men were less intelligent than their descendants today. Their best brains were just as good, and their indifferent ones just as indifferent as our own. They seem remote to us only because mankind, through untold centuries and thousands of years, has amassed knowledge about things his ancestors knew nothing of, and because his descendants through the ages have improved and added to the inventions of implements

and technical devices, wherewith man tried to make up for his
bodily frailty. Lacking feathers or pelts as protection against the
cold, lacking fangs and talons in the fight for survival against animals
of prey and the competition for vegetable food against horned and
hoofed beasts, he had to be sagacious and courageous, and also to be
co-operative within his small society of relatives and fellow-tribes-
men. He had to observe surrounding nature and find out how he
could utilize all powers that seemed friendly to him, avoid or pro-
pitiate inimical powers. Primitive men usually have keener powers
of observation than their more civilized descendants, and they use
their common sense and understanding, when they try to interpret
what they have observed. Even when their ways and ideas seem
strange and meaningless to us—as we used to imagine the behavior
of so-called savages was absurd and silly—primitive men always had
a meaning for everything they did—they could not afford not to.
Man has always had to live by his wits.

But lacking the body of knowledge that has been culled by the
experiences of untold generations about the nature of living and
lifeless matter—what we call natural laws—they very reasonably
concluded that everything in the environment of man was like himself, moved by reason that made for safety, or by passions that made
him run headlong into danger. Stones turned hot or cold, just as men
do; the trees bowed to the storm, animals loved their young ones and
were willing to die to defend them. The lightning was hurled out
from the clouds, rain pattered on the roof of the forest or whipped
the dust of the prairies, the ocean and the brook and the winds in the
woods had voices, different from the voices of the animals and the
language of man, but to primitive man it was natural to think that
they were saying something in their own language. To him all sounds
and sights and changes must appear as the willed expressions of somebody's anger or friendliness, desire or fear or will to self-defence.

So he came to believe in beings of another order than mankind. Sometimes he saw them, in his nightly dreams or in his visions of fever, or he just conjured them up by his expectant imagination. Spooks, spirits, ogres, trolls, fairies they have been called at different times. But the great forces that man knew his life depended upon—the sunlight and the rain, fair or foul weather—they came to worship as great or small gods. The Sun and the Moon and the Stars rose up from the bosom of the Earth that mothered all living things, wandered across the sky to return into her bosom again—or maybe they descended into a realm beneath the soil. All tribes and people seem to have believed in this subterranean world, even if their notions about what it was like differed.

Inborn in the soul of man seems to be a conviction that the force which makes men and beasts live and move, does escape and survive, when death has reduced the body to a powerless, rotting or edible matter. It was not a belief in life eternal; the spirits were usually held to wither away and disappear by and by. And the life of the bodiless spirits was usually pictured as a poor and miserable existence. The dead missed all the delightful things we enjoy with our senses. So the ghosts were envious of the living and malicious, and men feared them and tried to console them with burial rites and sacrifices to the dead, to make them less unfriendly. If the corpses were buried in the ground, the dead might have a chance in the underworld. Or, much later they believed that the burning of the corpses might help the ghosts to ascend to the realms of the sky, where the gods had their home.

Some scholars believe that all the creatures of popular fancy who inhabit the world under the ground, or inside the mountains, or the castles on the bottom of the ocean, were at first the dead—the ancestors. Because they are dead they cannot have children of their own but want to kidnap human babies and young people. And because they died such a long while ago they know nothing of the improved techniques of life which their descendants have evolved since their times. So the old man in the mountain, or the good fellow who has his farm underneath the farmer's byre are very pleased to get a hired man from the world of the living. The people of the underworld may have powers of their own—magic that bewilders men and changes the shapes and appearances of things. But in the tales it is usually human ingenuity that has the better of it, when man and troll meet.

III

His next of kin were the animals—man always knew that. In fact, at times he scarcely was aware that there was any difference between them and himself. Some of them might be his enemies, or his rivals for the food supplies he wanted to secure for himself. But even so, he was willing to believe that a bear or an eagle or a big fish had been the ancestor of his tribe, or that the spirit of dead people moved into the bodies of animals. His own spirit might enter a bird or a mammal or a snake, when his body lay asleep, and at night he might roam and take part in the life of the animal kingdom. Tales of marriages between men and beasts have been told among the Eskimos, neighbors of the North Pole, and among the jungle people of Africa or South America. The bear husband or the jaguar wife behave very much like other husbands and wives: they are jealous, affectionate or bad-tempered, fond parents or tyrannical parents. A later idea was that gods and fairies would appear in the shapes of animals which they could assume or shed at will. Still younger are the tales of swan maidens or seal girls who leave their hides on the beach whilst they bathe and play, and the fisherboy who steals one of the coats and takes the maiden home and makes her his wife. The supernatural being would make a good, obedient wife, but if she happened to discover where her husband had hidden her hide, she would don it and leave him and their children, to return to her own people. Primitive man never doubted that the animals, whose behavior was so perfectly adapted to their needs of food and security, lived by laws and rules, just as he had to do. They, too, must have their kings and gods and chieftains. The strongest, fiercest and most beautiful animals would be monarchs of the others. Though the highest rank was given to different animals in different parts of the world—while the lion was widely regarded as the king of beasts, in Norway the bear was called king of the forests—it seems that the regal nature of the eagle was recognized almost everywhere.

But notwithstanding his awe of the strongest and proudest among the beasts, man always had a special partiality for some small, feeble but agile and cunning creature—one who like himself was handicapped by nature in the battle of life, but like himself managed to get the better of his stronger, less wary enemies and his somewhat unreliable mighty friends—an animal who had to live by his wits, just as he had to do. The American Indians knew a number of stories about the coyote, the Hindu about the jackal or the monkey. In Africa the hero of the Negroes' animal stories might be the weazel or even the wonderfully clever spider. In Europe the people enjoyed stories about the sly fox, fondly giving him a Christian name like Reynard or Reinecke, or in Scandinavia, Mikkel. They gloated and chuckled over his infinite resourcefulness and his cheek, when he fooled the bear and the wolf and the poor geese, or even the farmer and his wife, with his glib talk. But if it happened now and then, that the trickster was tricked, by the stolid bear or the sagacious old barnyard cock or by an old goodwife, who would not be taken in by Mikkel's ruses, that too made a delightful story.

In fact, none of the folk tales seem to have been so universally enjoyed as the animal stories. On one side they merge into the fairy tales and stories of the supernatural, but on the other they become as homely as the gossip about our next-door neighbors and the jokes about the goings on in our own family. In a way they continue to live among us, adapted to another age and other means of telling them. That explains the immense popularity of Donald Duck, the Big Bad Wolf, Bingo, the dog, and all the other creatures of the moving pictures. They are very different from the old tales, in which everyone had personal experiences with his four-footed neighbors and treated them realistically even when they told the most fantastic stories about them. Children nowadays have scant opportunity to meet the wild animals of the forests; farming has largely become an industry and the old intimate relationship between the peasant and his barnyard folks has become businesslike. Yet, after all, real affection may still spring up between country people and some individual of their livestock, or between the driver and his horse, and children still love their pets, talk to them and imagine what Doggie or Pussy means to say—though I think most children today would be scared stiff if the puppy or the cat started talking back. Their ancestors some generations back would have thought it perfectly natural. And that, perhaps, more than anything else, will make us see how far we have travelled from the world where the folk tales were born and grew and changed, until they assumed the shapes they had, when they were first written down by collectors.

IV

THROUGHOUT the ages, when the old tales were handed down from generation to generation by word of mouth, they were not thought of as stories for the children. No doubt the children of the tribesmen tried to slip in among the listeners—unless some grownups chased them away—when a storyteller of local renown started an evening's entertainment. And no doubt many of the tales were told the children by their parents or their grandparents; that was part of their education. For in the stories were embodied their belief in gods and powers, their thoughts of life and death, the wisdom of the ancients, and the common sense of everyday people. They were the poetry, and the flight into fiction too, of people who had not yet invented the art of writing as a means of storing up the treasures of culture that their forefathers had created and handed down to them. The priests recited them when the tribe gathered for sacrifices and religious rites: the teachers told them to their students; the huntsmen and the shepherds told them when they lay down by the campfire, under the starry skies of the plains. And the young people entertained each other with moving or ribald tales, when they met and had a good time.

When the people of Asia, who first built cities and evolved a complex civilization, discovered writing, the tales soon made their way into the written lore of the nations. But that did not impair their vitality. They continued to live their old life on the lips of men and women. Professional storytellers made a living from rapt audiences. According to legends, a doomed princess saved her life by telling stories through one thousand and one nights, and captives won their liberty and the favor of irate kings by storytelling. When waves of culture surged from the East toward the West and fertilized the minds of the still primitive people of Europe, the folklore of the Orient was made known and lapped up avidly by fresh minds who blended the foreign stuff with their own legends, or re-molded it according to their own tastes. The world of marvels and supernatural beings, created by the exuberant imagination of the Eastern nations—by now a magic carpet of wonderful richness and glowing colors—inspired the poets of the Greek and Roman world, and the old tales were given new shapes and new meanings.

A favorite subject of the Orientals had been the loves of gods and goddesses or fairies, for human boys and girls. When Apuleius, the Latin poet, fashioned his pretty tale about the love of Psyche, the soul, and Cupid, god of Love, the stuff he used no doubt was widely known among the common people, from a hundred tales—about the evil mother-in-law, the trials of true lovers, the impossible tasks which a poor human being is enabled to carry out with the help of friendly animals! Though Apuleius' refined use of the stories as a parable of how Love makes the Soul immortal and the peer of the gods was written for a public of highbrow litterati, his rendering of the trials of the mortal bride of a supernatural bridegroom has left its marks on the folk tales of many lands. The Norwegian story, "East of the Sun and West of the Moon," keeps very close in the footsteps of Apuleius, though it is shorter and more dramatic. The idea that the human lover will lose his or her supernatural love if the admonition to secrecy is violated, runs through all these stories. According to the popular ideas about the behavior of the sexes, when the bride is human, she usually lets herself be betrayed by her curiosity; but when the story is about a man and his supernatural bride, he falls because of the temptation to boast of his wife's beauty and the splendors of his home in fairyland. Boasting leads to the temporary loss of his fairy queen for the knights in Breton and Irish medieval poems, as it does to Halvor of "Soria Moria Castle" or to the bridegroom of the "Princess from Whitelands."

But sometimes the fairy bride or the giant husband, unhampered by the notions about right and wrong that humanity must live by, are a puzzle or a terror to their mortal spouses. The Greeks, who wanted their gods and fairies lifelike and realistic too, even made

Medea, the sorceress, into a mortal—she is wild and unbridled in her passions of love and hatred, because she is the daughter of an alien, barbaric race. Her husband, Jason, mean and calculating, still seemed to them a fair representative of their own people, since he lets reason rule his actions. But no doubt Medea has once been a creature from another world than ours. "The Mastermaid" in this book is her younger sister, considerably less fierce, even if she, too, in her loyalty to her lover, treats the unwanted suitors rather brutally. The tale of "The Mastermaid" has been a great favorite among Nordic people, and collectors have taken down more than a hundred different renderings of it from the lips of old wives and old men. There was a tendency to soften or cut out the part about the heroine's heartlessness towards everybody but her lover. In one Norse version, "Randi on the Stone," and in a lovely Danish one called "The Forgotten Sweetheart," nothing is left except the resourcefulness and the tender and patient faith of the girl from the nether world. Asbjørnsen and Moe, when they first edited their manuscripts, preferred "The Mastermaid" as it is printed here, because they believed that this is an older form, and they probably were right.

It seems that most of these folk tales were already known all over Europe in the Middle Ages, at least in their general outlines. They were spread abroad by minstrels and jesters and by the pilgrims who travelled all over the bad roads of the times. For even if the pilgrims of the Middle Ages made their voyages for the sake of piety, it was the only kind of tourism that was known to them, and the only way they had to go on vacations. So they sometimes tired of praying and hearing edifying stories and wanted to relax in hostels or inns. It was quite natural then that much of the stuff of the fairy tales should also seep into the legends of the Saints. The tale of the king who wants to marry his own daughter and of how the daughter in vain tries to make him give up his wicked plan by demanding impossible gifts, until she has to flee from home disguised as a beggar maiden, has become part of the legend of St. Dympna, an Irish Saint who is buried near Gheel in Flanders and venerated as the patron saint of feeble-minded children. In France the princess became the famous because she dressed in the hide of the ass who made gold—the precious source of State revenue—that her father killed at her request. The story of Grimm about "The Girl without Hands," maimed by her wicked mother-in-law and turned out in the wilderness with her baby tied to her bosom, occurs in a medieval Swedish collection of legends as the history of the mother of St. Bartholomew, the Apostle—for though you would never guess it from the mention made of St. Bartholomew in the New Testament—according to the ancient Swedes, he was the son of an Oriental king.

Some of the stories with a homely moral, like the one called "The Reward of the World," were told by preachers who wanted to draw the attention of their congregations to fundamental truths by lively illustrations. The Dominican Fathers even made collections of witty short stories and succinct parables suited for this purpose.

In the Norse folktales there are few traces of the religion of the gods of Valhall, as we know them from the myths of the Eddas. To the common people the high gods always seemed rather remote. The part of their religion that really mattered was the belief in minor gods and elves who lived on the soil of the farm and beneath the house and in the lakes and hills near home, and had to be kept friendly by sacrifices and all kinds of attentions. This homely paganism survived all the attempts of Catholic and Lutheran priests to eradicate it. The Norsemen became good Christians, but secretly they still put out the dish of porridge to the Puck in the stable, and beer on the burial mound of the ancestors. Some of these supernatural beings withered away more quickly than others. The belief in the trolls cannot have been very great even in the Saga times, for in the

"Lying Sagas" (which is the Old Norse name for fiction as distinct from historical sagas) the trolls are treated with a lack of reverence that would be incompatible with the fear of the dwellers of the wild mountains of Norway. Others have survived until electric light and motorized farming made them homeless in the countryside. And in the fairy tales Thursday night—the day of Thor—is the time when all kinds of spooks and uncanny things are on the loose.

Traces of the Catholic past of the Scandinavian countries are to be found in the tales about Our Lord and St. Peter wandering on Earth and having all kinds of adventures; of the Virgin Mary; and also of the Devil, who in the tales usually is regarded as none too bright. He can never be sure to bag the soul of a sinner, even if he has a perfectly valid signed contract for it—unless of course it is the soul of a skinflint lawyer or a crooked sheriff, which neither God nor men would want to deprive him of. Many of the stories that make fun of the clergy also date back to Catholic times, though the priest has become a parson, dressed in the black gown and white ruff of the Lutheran minister, and for companion he has been given the latter-day ecclesiastical functionary, the sexton, who in Norway was also the village schoolmaster and regarded by the peasants as a man who knew a thing or two besides the Lord's Prayer.

For in their leisurely way the folk tales also moved with the times. As new customs, new trades and new inventions appeared in the country, they also appeared in the stories. The charmed weapon of olden times became a rifle that hits whatever it is aimed at: the flutes of Pan and the lute of Orpheus turned into a whistle that called men and animals to heel, and the fiddle of Little Frikk. The troll and the witches develop tastes for brandy and chewing tobacco, and the hard-boiled skipper makes the Devil work a tolerably modern suction pump, of which poor Old Nick evidently did not understand a thing.

But the stories not only had to adapt themselves to the times, they had to make themselves at home in every country they came to. So although the Norwegian folk tales have wandered far and wide through space and time, to us Norwegians they seem to be blood of our own blood, and bone of our own bone, as homely as our mountains and forests and fjords. It is our way of looking at life and judging people, they express. We never liked glamor, we always thought it rather vulgar—real life with its troubles and jokes and sorrows and joys was good enough for us, and even when we day-dreamed, we dreamed of a world not too unlike the one we knew and loved. Fairy tales like the Irish or the French, we never had. The creation of our fancy that came nearest to a fairy was the "Hulder," and she is a buxom girl, heir to a large farm in the underworld, boy-crazy but handsome—only, she has a tail like a cow. The king of the folk tales does not live in a moated and turreted castle but in a "kongsgård,"—literally the "king's farm," even if it is a glorified manor farm like the ones where the old and wealthy rural families have lived for centuries and ruled the countryside as arrogantly and arbitrarily as any lord or baron abroad. The king's daughter is just the spoiled heiress, or the dignified and refined young girl of this rural aristocracy, and it does not make much difference, whether her father is a king above or beneath the green fields. The moral of the folk tales—for the Norwegian folk tales are usually very moral—is the moral our country people believed in: the kind and the gener-ous, the brave and the sincere, will get their rewards in the end. The good stepdaughter who even steps gingerly over the brushwood fence, careful not to hurt a twig, is given beauty and riches, but the bad girl who handles dead and living things equally brutally, will get a box full of snakes that kill her. When True overhears the palaver of the animals beneath the lime tree where he has found refuge for the night, they lead him to restored sight and a princess for his bride;

to Untrue they bring death. But the favorite hero of the Norwegian folk tales is Espen Ashlad, the youth who seems too indolent and lazy to do anything but sit in the inglenook the livelong day. He embodies a wishful dream of the Norwegians, hardworking on their stony soil and along the storm-swept coast. Wouldn't it be a fine thing, if a man could take life easy most of the time and yet come out on top, when he was faced with a difficult or dangerous task, doing ever so much better than all the self-important and careworn drudges who always want the young people to work like slaves? No, Espen Ashlad is a deep one, sly and canny, but he is also courageous and resourceful in a difficult situation. He may be ruthless when he has to deal with a cussed king or dumb trolls, but he is kind to the poor and the old, ever willing to help those who seemingly would never be able to do anything for him in return. So he shall have his reward. The story may waive this strictly moral attitude when the hero is a master thief, or a poor lad who has to use his wits to get along in the world in spite of severe handicaps, but then their victims are always people who did not deserve better.

Though the storytellers never go in for word-painting of the scenery, the whole nature of Norway is in the folk tales. Storms rage in the North Sea and the breakers thunder along the shores, leaving the shipwrecked sailor marooned on the island where the Big Bird Dam has his home. High above the timber line are the upland fells where Dapplegrim was reared. Through the endless forests the wanderer has to travel, down into one valley and uphill and down again, until he has lost his bearings, but at last he will see the faraway pale blue ridge, where lies his goal. The old crony who lives in the midst of the woods in her tiny hut is more used to talking to the wild animals and the birds and the Moon and the Winds than to seeing human visitors. On the crest of the slope is the stately manor farm, surrounded by fields and pastures, where sleek fat cattle and fine horses graze, and the weary wanderer jogs on, hopeful that here he will be given a full meal at nightfall and a soft bed to sleep in. The people go about their business, tilling the soil, caring for their cattle, felling timber or looking after their nets and their boats—and then they sail or walk or tumble down a hole in the field, right into the realm of the supernatural, where after a while they will feel very much at home. It is rather like the world they came from.

V

THE age of the New Learning—the revival of the study of Greek and classical Latin, the discoveries that opened up new continents to the voyagers from Europe and a new understanding of the laws of nature that encouraged scientific research—made the old tales lose much of their attraction for the grownups of the educated classes. They seemed so crude and full of superstitions, their language was unrefined, their morals unsophisticated! They were good enough for the common people, who could not read books and that intriguing novelty, the newspapers; and for the children who heard them from their nurses and the servants who loved them—children were so naïve.

Even so, it might happen that some of these children cherished the memory of their nurse's stories, long after he or she had become an erudite gentleman or a refined lady. Monsieur Charles Perrault, who was an important member of the Ministry of Finance in Paris in the time of King Louis XIV, and also dabbled in poetry, conceived the idea of writing down some of the stories he remembered as entertaining and not devoid of charm. "Mother Goose's Tales," he called his slim volume. It is a delightful book, or at least I thought so when I was a child, and I still think so. Cinderella, Bluebeard's silly wife, the master of Puss in Boots and the Sleeping Beauty, not to mention those ladylike French fairies, are such charmingly polite and nice-mannered people. If you have read Perrault at an early age you will have learned how bad it really is to be bad-mannered, lacking in courtesy and kindness—only ogres behave that way. The ladies Madame d'Aulnaye and Madame Leprince de Beaumont followed in his steps, but they overdid the refinement. Yet the latter was the first to write down the tale of "Beauty and the Beast."

The Age of Enlightenment lasted until the people got a little tired of their classics and discovered that erudite persons easily become bores, fussy and musty. The Romantic movement wanted to return to the grassroots—among a lot of other things between heaven and earth they wanted to explore. They believed in the wisdom of common men, "the merry sons of Nature," in the pure and unbiased outlook of young children. From the common men, "The People," they hoped to win an understanding of the true mind and temper of their national stock. For centuries the historians had been interested in the deeds of kings and war lords, of philosophers and politicians, now they started researches into the lives and customs of the common folk. One great truth they discovered—that from the superstitions of the peasants and workingmen they might excavate the spiritual history of humanity. By digging after the roots of the languages they would learn a lot about the great movements of mankind, that flowed like a groundswell beneath the history of kingdoms and dynasties and wars and schools of philosophy and learning.

In the beginning of the nineteenth century a great German scholar, Jacob Grimm, devoted his penetrating intellect and his immense learning and industry to the study of the language and the laws and the ancient literature of his own and the neighboring countries. As a part of this lifework he collected, in collaboration with his brother, Wilhelm, the German "The Children's and the Home's

Tales." The work of Jacob Grimm became a source of inspiration to scholars of all the civilized countries; to linguists, historians, students of the arts and crafts of many nations. Fitfully and planlessly lovers of the old lore had already collected popular ballads and music from many lands, England and Scotland among others. Now this gleaning of the poetry of the people became systematized. Many systems evolved, and a new science called "Folklore" was born. The wave of enthusiasm that Grimm started has never abated. The work of the folklorists has long ago embraced the whole of our globe, and from the unwritten poetry and wisdom of the people our forefathers called savages, we have learned to understand and value human genius and the courageous conquest by man of his environment, as well as of his own mind. These achievements are not confined to any race and any age; they are the brief of our universal brotherhood of man.

In 1842 the great Jacob Grimm received, from two young Norwegian students, a volume of Norwegian folk tales, gathered from the lips of the peasants. One, Jørgen Moe, was the son of an old rural family who for centuries had owned the great farm of Moe on Ringerike (near Oslo). The other, P. Chr. Asbjørnsen, was from Christiania, as Oslo was called at that time. His father was a well-to-do artisan and owner of a rambling old house in the suburbs, teeming with servants and with spooks, too. The lads had met, when they were both boarded with a parson on Ringerike who was supposed to coach them for their entrance to the University of Christiania.

Grimm was enthusiastic about the work of the two youths; he had scarcely ever seen a collection where the meaty stuff and the vivid style of the old storytellers had been rendered with greater perfection. The judgment of the great master has never seriously been disputed, even if some Norwegian ladies, to begin with, objected to the "crudeness"—they would have liked the stories told more in the style of the French collectors. But the fact was, both Jørgen Moe and Asbjørnsen were poets in their own right. They had a fine sense of the oral style of the countrymen, and for all the Scandinavian countries they laid down, once and for all times, the proper way of editing folk tales—unadorned with frills and frippery, gay or serious, but simple and straightforward always.

Jørgen Moe became a parson and a bishop, and by and by he withdrew from the work on the folk tales. He wrote some exquisite lyrical poetry, and two volumes of stories for children—mainly based on the memories of his own and his little sister's childhood. To Norwegian children they are as dear as the March girls or Tom Sawyer to young America. When he died, in 1882, all Norway mourned him as a fine poet and an exceedingly lovable character.

Peter Christian Asbjørnsen studied forestry in Germany, but he had far too many interests and hobbies ever to settle down to a regular job of any kind. He travelled all over the country in search of folk tales and wrote some volumes about his travelling adventures and the strange or funny or charming people he had met and hobnobbed with. Few men have loved the nature of Norway as he did, or written about it as beautifully as Asbjørnsen. He was a passionate fisher and hunter, loved good food and wrote books about cookery and "sensible housekeeping." Those books brought the good old-fashioned Norwegian housewives up in arms against him, this "man who would mind the house!" He lived and died a bachelor, spending his last years in a ramshackle old frame house in a great garden in a suburb of Oslo. His apartment was filled with books and paintings, gifts from his numerous artist friends, and Asbjørnsen puttered around and prepared with his own hands the delicious food he served his visitors. An immense number of stories and anecdotes survive him. He died when I was a small girl—I do not remember the year—but we children never walked past "Asbjørnsen's house" without feeling that this was a shrine from which the most precious gifts had been lavished on all of us.

Sigrid Undset

TRUE AND UNTRUE

* * *

ONCE on a time there were two brothers; one was called True, and the other Untrue. True was always upright and good towards all, but Untrue was bad and full of lies, so that no one could believe what he said. Their mother was a widow, and hadn't much to live on; so when her sons had grown up, she was forced to send them away to earn their bread in the world. Each took a little scrip with some food in it, and then they went their way.

Now, when they had walked till evening, they sat down on a windfall in the wood, and took out their scrips, for they were hungry after walking the whole day and thought a morsel of food would be sweet enough.

"If you're of my mind," said Untrue, "I think we had better eat out of your scrip, so long as there is anything in it, and after that we can take to mine."

Yes! True was well pleased with this, so they fell to eating, but Untrue got all the best bits, and stuffed himself with them, while True got only the burnt crusts and scraps.

Next morning they broke their fast with True's food, and they dined on it too, and then there was nothing left in his scrip. So when they had walked till late at night, and were ready to eat again, True wanted to eat out of his brother's scrip, but Untrue said, "No," the food was his, and he had only enough for himself.

"Nay! but you know you ate out of my scrip so long as there was anything in it," said True.

"All very fine, I dare say," answered Untrue; "but if you are such a fool as to let others eat up your food before your face, you must make the best of it; for now all you have to do is to sit here and starve."

"Very well!" said True, "you're Untrue by name and untrue by nature; so you have been, and so you will be all your life long."

Now when Untrue heard this, he flew into a rage, and rushed at his brother, and plucked out both his eyes. "Now, try to see whether folk are untrue or not, you blind buzzard!" And so saying, he ran away and left him.

Poor True! There he went walking along and feeling his way through the thick wood. Blind and alone, he scarcely knew which way to turn, when all at once he caught hold of the trunk of a great bushy lime tree. He thought he would climb up into it, and sit there till the night was over for fear of the wild beasts.

"When the birds begin to sing," he said to himself, "then I shall know it is day, and I can try to grope my way farther on." So he climbed up into the lime tree. After he had sat there a little time, he heard someone stirring and clattering under the tree, and soon after others came; and when they began to greet one another, he found that it was Bruin, the bear, and Greylegs, the wolf, and Slyboots, the fox, and Longears, the hare, who had come to keep St. John's Eve under the tree. So they began to eat and drink, and be merry; and when they had done eating, they fell to gossiping together. At last the Fox said:

"Shan't we, each of us, tell a little story while we sit here?"

Well! the others had nothing against that. It would be good fun, they said, and the bear began; for you may fancy he was king of the company.

"The King of England," said Bruin, "has such bad eyesight, he can scarcely see a yard before him; but if he only came to this lime tree in the morning, while the dew is still on the leaves, and rubbed his eyes with the dew, he would get back his sight as good as ever."

"Very true!" said Greylegs. "The King of England has a deaf and dumb daughter too; but if he only knew what I know, he would soon cure her. Last year she went to communion. She let a crumb of the bread fall out of her mouth, and a great toad came and swallowed it down; but if they only dug up the chancel floor, they would find the toad sitting right under the altar rails, with the bread sticking in his throat. If they were to cut the toad open and give the bread to the princess, she would be like other folk again as to her speech and hearing."

"That's all very well," said the fox; "but if the King of England knew what I know, he would not be so badly off for water in his palace; for under the great stone, in his palace yard, is a spring of the clearest water one could wish for, if he only knew to dig for it there."

"Ah!" said the hare in a small voice; "the King of England has the finest orchard in the whole land, but it does not bear so much as a crab, for there lies a heavy gold chain in three turns round the orchard. If he had that dug up, there would not be a garden like it for bearing fruit, in all his kingdom."

"Very true, I dare say," said the fox; "but now it's getting very late, and we may as well go home."

So they all went away together.

After they were gone, True fell asleep up in the tree; but when the birds began to sing at dawn, he woke up, and took the dew from the leaves, and rubbed his eyes with it, and so got his sight back as good as it was before Untrue plucked his eyes out.

Then he went straight to the King of England's palace, and begged for work, and got it on the spot. So one day the King came out into the palace yard, and when he had walked about a bit, he wanted to drink out of his pump; for you must know the day was hot, and the King very thirsty; but when they poured him out a glass, it was so muddy, and nasty, and foul, that the King got quite vexed.

"I don't think there's ever a man in my whole kingdom who has such bad water in his yard as I, and yet I bring it in pipes from afar, over hill and dale," cried out the King.

"Like enough, your Majesty," said True, "but if you would let me have some men to help me to dig up this great stone which lies here in the middle of your yard, you would soon see good water, and plenty of it."

Well! the King was willing enough; and they had scarcely got the stone well out, and dug under it a while, before a jet of water sprang out high up into the air, as clear and full as if it came out of a conduit, and clearer water was not to be found in all England.

A little while after the King was out in his palace yard again, and there came a great hawk flying after his chickens, and all the King's men began to clap their hands and bawl out, "There he flies!"

"There he flies!" The King caught up his gun and tried to shoot the hawk, but he couldn't see so far, so he fell into great grief.

"Would to Heaven," he said, "there was someone who could tell me a cure for my eyes; for I think I shall soon go quite blind!"

"I can tell you one soon enough," said True; and then he told the King what he had done to cure his own eyes, and the King set off that very afternoon to the lime tree, as you may fancy, and his eyes were quite cured as soon as he rubbed them with the dew which was on the leaves in the morning. From that time forth there was no one whom the King held so dear as True, and he had to be with him wherever he went, both at home and abroad.

So one day, as they were walking together in the orchard, the King said, "There isn't a man in England who spends so much on his orchard as I and yet I can't get one of the trees to bear so much as a crab."

"Well, well!" said True; "if I may have what lies three times twisted round your orchard, and men to dig it up, your orchard will bear well enough."

Yes, the King was quite willing, so True got men and began to dig, and at last he dug up the whole gold chain. Now True was a rich man, far richer indeed than the King himself; but still the King was well pleased, for his orchard bore so that the boughs of the trees hung down to the ground, and such sweet apples and pears nobody had ever tasted.

Another day, too, the King and True were walking about, and talking together, when the Princess passed them, and the King was quite downcast when he saw her.

"Isn't it a pity, now, that so lovely a Princess as mine should want speech and hearing?" he said to True.

"Ay, but there is a cure for that," said True.

When the King heard that, he was so glad that he promised him the Princess to wife, and half his kingdom into the bargain, if he could get her right again. So True took a few men, and went into the church and dug up the toad which sat under the altar rails. Then he cut open the toad, and took out the bread and gave it to the King's daughter; and from that hour she got back her speech, and could talk like other people.

Now True was to have the Princess, and they got ready for the bridal feast. Such a feast had never been seen before; it was the talk of the whole land. Just as they were in the midst of dancing the bridal dance, in came a beggar lad, and begged for a morsel of food, and he was so ragged and wretched that every one crossed himself

when they looked at him; but True knew him at once, and saw that it was Untrue, his brother.

"Do you know me again?" said True.

"Oh! where should such a one as I ever have seen so great a lord?" said Untrue.

"Still, you have seen me before," said True. "It was I whose eyes you plucked out a year ago this very day. Untrue by name, and untrue by nature; so I said before, and so I say now. But you are still my brother, and so you shall have some food. After that, you may go to the lime tree where I sat last year; if you hear anything that can do you good, you will be lucky."

So Untrue did not wait to be told twice. "If True has got so much good by sitting in the lime tree, that in one year he has come to be king over half England, what good may I not get?" he thought. So he set off and climbed up into the lime tree. He had not sat there long, before all the beasts came as before, and ate and drank, and kept St. John's Eve under the tree. When they had left off eating, the fox wished that they would begin to tell stories, and Untrue got ready to listen with all his might, till his ears were almost fit to fall off. But Bruin, the bear, was surly, and growled and said:

"Some one has been chattering about what we said last year, and so now we will hold our tongues about what we know." And with that the beasts bade one another good night, and parted, and Untrue was just as wise as he was before, and the reason was that his name was Untrue, and his nature untrue too.

THE MASTERMAID

* * *

ONCE on a time there was a king who had several sons—I don't
know how many there were—but the youngest had no rest at home,
for nothing else would please him but to go out into the world and
try his luck, and after a long time the king was forced to give him
leave to go. Now, after he had travelled some days, he came one
night to a Giant's house, and there he got a place in the Giant's service. In the morning the Giant went off to herd his goats, and as he
left the yard, he told the Prince to clean out the stable; "and after
you have done that, you needn't do anything else today; for you must
know it is an easy master you have come to. But what is set you to
do you must do well, and you mustn't think of going into any of the
rooms which are beyond that in which you slept, for if you do, I'll
take your life."

"Sure enough, it is an easy master I have got," said the Prince to
himself, as he walked up and down the room, and carolled and sang,
for he thought there was plenty of time to clean out the stable.

"But still it would be good fun just to peep into his other rooms,
for there must be something in them which he is afraid lest I should
see, since he won't give me leave to go in."

So he went into the first room, and there was a pot boiling on a hook by the wall, but the Prince saw no fire underneath it. "I wonder what is inside it," he thought; and then he dipped a lock of his hair into it, and the hair seemed as if it were all turned to copper.

"What a dainty broth," he said; "if one tasted, he'd look grand inside his gullet"; and with that he went into the next room. There, too, was a pot hanging by a hook, which bubbled and boiled; but there was no fire under that either.

"I may as well try this too," said the Prince, as he put another lock into the pot, and it came out all silvered.

"They haven't such rich broth in my father's house," said the Prince; "but it all depends on how it tastes," and with that he went on into the third room. There, too, hung a pot that boiled just like those he had seen in the two other rooms; and the Prince had a mind to try this too, so he dipped a lock of hair into it, and it came out gilded, so that the light gleamed from it.

"'Worse and worse,' said the old wife; but I say better and better," said the Prince; "but if he boils gold here, I wonder what he boils in yonder room."

He thought he might as well see; so he went through the door into the fourth room. Well, there was no pot in there, but there was a Princess, seated on a bench, so lovely, that the Prince had never seen anyone like her in all his born days.

"Oh! in Heaven's name," she said, "what do you want here?"

"I got a place here yesterday," said the Prince.

"A place, indeed! Heaven help you out of it."

"Well, after all, I think I've got an easy master; he hasn't set me much to do today, for after I have cleaned out the stable, my day's work is over."

"Yes, but how will you do it?" she said; "for if you set to work to clean it like other folk, ten pitchforks full will come in for every one you toss out. But I will teach you how to set to work; you must turn the fork upside down, and toss with the handle, and then all the dung will fly out of itself."

Yes, he would be sure to do that, said the Prince; and so he sat there the whole day, for he and Princess were soon great friends, and had made up their minds to have one another. And so the first day of his service with the Giant was not long, as you may fancy. But when the evening drew on, she said it would be as well if he got the stable cleaned out before the Giant came home. When he went to the stable, he thought he would just see if what she had said were true, and so he began to work like the grooms in his father's stable. But he soon had enough of that, for he hadn't worked a minute before the stable was so full of dung that he hadn't room to stand. Then he did as the Princess bade him, and turned up the fork and worked with the handle, and lo! in a trice the stable was as clean as if it had been scoured. And when he had done his work, he went back into the room where the Giant had given him leave to be, and began to walk up and down, and to carol and sing. So after a bit, home came the Giant with his goats.

"Have you cleaned the stable?" asked the Giant.

"Yes, now it's all right and tight, master," answered the Prince.

"I'll soon see if it is," growled the Giant, and strode off to the stable, where he found it just as the Prince had said.

"You've been talking to my Mastermaid, I can see," said the Giant; "for you've not sucked this knowledge out of your own breast."

"Mastermaid," said the Prince, who looked as stupid as an owl. "What sort of thing is that master? I'd be very glad to see it."

"Well, well!" said the Giant, "you'll see her soon enough."

Next day the Giant set off with his goats again, and before he went he told the Prince to fetch home his horse, which was out at grass on the hillside, and when he had done that he might rest all day.

"For you must know, it is an easy master you have come to," said the Giant. "But if you go into any of the rooms I spoke of yesterday, I'll wring your head off."

So off he went with his flock of goats.

"An easy master you are indeed," said the Prince; "but for all that, I'll just go in and have a chat with your Mastermaid; maybe she would as soon be mine as yours." So he went in to her, and she asked him what he had to do that day.

"Oh! nothing to be afraid of," said he. "I've only to go up to the hillside to fetch his horse."

"Very well, and how will you set about it?"

"Well, for that matter, there's no great art in riding a horse home. I fancy I've ridden fresher horses before now," said the Prince.

"Ah, but this isn't so easy a task as you think; but I'll teach you how to do it. When you get near it, fire and flame will come out of its nostrils, as out of a tar barrel; but look out, and take the bit which hangs behind the door yonder, and throw it right into his jaws, and he will grow so tame that you may do what you like with him."

Yes! the Prince would mind and do that; and so he sat in there the whole day, talking and chatting with the Mastermaid about one thing and another, but they always came back to how happy they would be if they could only have one another, and get well away from the Giant. And to tell the truth, the Prince would have clean forgotten both the horse and the hillside, if the Mastermaid hadn't put him in mind of them when evening drew on, telling him he had better set out to fetch the horse before the Giant came home. So he set off, and took the bit which hung in the corner, ran up the hill, and it wasn't long before he met the horse, with fire and flame streaming out of its nostrils. But he watched his chance, and, as the horse came open-jawed up to him, he threw the bit into its mouth, and it stood as quiet as a lamb. After that, it was no great matter to ride it home and put it up, you may fancy; and then the Prince went into his room again, and began to carol and sing.

So the Giant came home again at even with his goats; and the first words he said were,

"Have you brought my horse down from the hill?"

"Yes, master, that I have," said the Prince; "and a better horse I never bestrode; but for all that I rode him straight home, and put him up safe and sound."

"I'll soon see to that," said the Giant, and ran out to the stable, and there stood the horse just as the Prince had said.

"You've talked to my Mastermaid, I'll be bound, for you haven't sucked this out of your own breast," said the Giant again.

"Yesterday master talked of this Mastermaid, and today it's the same story," said the Prince, who pretended to be silly and stupid. "Bless you, master! Why don't you show me the thing at once? I should so like to see it only once in my life."

"Oh, if that's all," said the Giant, "you'll see her soon enough."

The third day, at dawn, the Giant went off to the wood again with his goats; but before he went he said to the Prince, "Today you must go to Hell and fetch my subsidies. When you have done that you can rest yourself all day, for you must know it is an easy master you have come to," and with that off he went.

"Easy master, indeed!" said the Prince. "You may be easy, but you set me hard tasks all the same. But I may as well see if I can find your Mastermaid, as you call her. I daresay she'll tell me what to do"; and so in he went to her again.

So when the Mastermaid asked what the Giant had set him to do that day, he told her how he was to go to Hell and fetch the subsidies.

"And how will you set about it?" asked the Mastermaid.

"Oh, that you must tell me," said the Prince. "I have never been to Hell in my life; and even if I knew the way, I don't know how much I am to ask for."

"Well, I'll soon tell you," said Mastermaid. "You must go to the steep rock away yonder, under the hillside, and take the club that lies there, and knock on the face of the rock. Then there will come out one, all glistening with fire; to him you must tell your errand; and when he asks you how much you will have, mind you say, 'As much as I can carry.'"

Yes, he would be sure to say that; so he sat in there with the Mastermaid all that day too; and though evening drew on, he would have sat there till now, had not the Mastermaid put him in mind that it was high time to be off to Hell to fetch the Giant's subsidies before he came home. So he went on his way, and did just as the Master-maid had told him; and when he reached the rock, he took up the club and gave a great thump. Then the rocks opened, and out came one whose face glistened, and out of whose eyes flew sparks of fire.

"What is your will?" said he.

"Oh! I'm only come from the Giant to fetch his subsidies," said the Prince.

"How much will you have then?" said the other.

"I never wish for more than I am able to carry," said the Prince.

"Lucky for you that you did not ask for a whole horseload," said he who came out of the rock. "But come now into the rock with me, and you shall have it."

So the Prince went in with him, and you may fancy what heaps and heaps of gold and silver he saw lying in there, just like stones in a gravel pit; and he got a load just as big as he was able to carry, and set off for home with it. Now, when the Giant came home with his goats at even, the Prince went into his room, and began to carol and sing as he had done the evenings before.

"Have you been to Hell after my subsidies?" roared the Giant.

"Oh, yes; that I have, master," answered the Prince.

"Where have you put it?" said the Giant.

"There stands the sack on the bench yonder," said the Prince.

"I'll soon see to that," said the Giant, who strode off to the bench, and there he saw the sack so full that the gold and silver dropped out on the floor as soon as ever he untied the string.

"You've been talking to my Mastermaid, that I can see," said the Giant; "but if you have, I'll wring your head off."

"Mastermaid!" said the Prince; "yesterday master talked of this Mastermaid, and today he talks of her again, and the day before yesterday it was the same story. I only wish I could see what sort of thing she is! That I do."

"Well, well, wait till tomorrow," said the Giant, "and then I'll take you in to her myself."

"Thank you kindly, master," said the Prince; "but it's only a joke of master's, I'll be bound."

So next day the Giant took him in to the Mastermaid, and said to her,

"Now, you must cut his throat, and boil him in the great big pot you wot of; and when the broth is ready, just give me a call."

After that, he laid him down on the bench to sleep, and began to snore so, that it sounded like thunder on the hills.

So the Mastermaid took a knife and cut the Prince in his little finger, and let three drops of blood fall on a three-legged stool; and after that she took all the old rags, and soles of shoes, and all the rubbish she could lay hands on, and put them into the pot; and then she filled a chest full of ground gold, and took a lump of salt, and a flask of water that hung behind the door, and she took, besides, a golden apple, and two golden chickens, and oft she set with the Prince from the Giant's house as fast as they could. And when they had gone a little way, they came to the sea, and sailed over it. But where they got the ship from, I have never heard tell.

So when the Giant had slumbered a good bit, he began to stretch himself as he lay on the bench, and called out, "Will it be soon done?"

"Only just begun," answered the first drop of blood on the stool.

So the Giant lay down to sleep again, and slumbered a long, long time. At last he began to toss about a little, and cried out,

"Do you hear what I say; will it be soon done?" but he did not look up this time, any more than the first, for he was still half asleep.

"Half done," said the second drop of blood.

Then the Giant thought again it was the Mastermaid, so he turned over on his other side, and fell asleep again; and when he had gone on sleeping for many hours, he began to stir and stretch his old bones, and to call out,

"Isn't it done yet?"

"Done to a turn," said the third drop of blood.

Then the Giant rose up and began to rub his eyes, but he couldn't see who it was that was talking to him, so he searched and called for the Mastermaid, but no one answered.

"Ah, well! I dare say she's just run out of doors for a bit," he thought, and took up a spoon and went up to the pot to taste the broth. But he found nothing but shoe-soles, and rags, and such stuff; and it was all boiled up together, so that he couldn't tell which was thick and which was thin. As soon as he saw this, he could tell how things had gone, and he got so angry he scarce knew which leg to stand upon. Away he went after the Prince and the Mastermaid, till the wind whistled behind him; but before long he came to the water and couldn't cross it.

"Never mind," he said; "I know a cure for this. I've only got to call on my stream-sucker."

So he called on his stream-sucker, and he came and stooped down, and took one, two, three gulps; and then so much water fell in the sea, that the Giant could see the Mastermaid and the Prince sailing in their ship.

"Now, you must cast out the lump of salt," said the Mastermaid.

So the Prince threw it overboard, and it grew up into a mountain so high, right across the sea, that the Giant couldn't pass it, and the stream-sucker couldn't help him by swilling any more water.

"Never mind!" cried the Giant; "there's a cure for this too." So he called on his hill-borer to come and bore through the mountain, that the stream-sucker might creep through and take another swill; but just as they had made a hole through the hill, and the stream-sucker was about to drink, the Mastermaid told the Prince to throw overboard a drop or two out of the flask, and then the sea was just as full as ever, and before the stream-sucker could take another gulp, they reached the land and were saved from the Giant.

So they made up their minds to go home to the Prince's father, but the Prince would not hear of the Mastermaid's walking for he thought it seemly neither for her nor for him.

"Just wait here ten minutes," he said, "while I go home after the seven horses which stand in my father's stall. It's no great way off, and I shan't be long about it; but I will not hear of my sweetheart walking to my father's palace."

"Ah!" said the Mastermaid, "pray don't leave me, for if you once get home to the palace, you'll forget me outright; I know you will."

"Oh!" said he, "how can I forget you; you with whom I have gone through so much, and whom I love so dearly?"

There was no help for it, he must and would go home to fetch the coach and seven horses, and she was to wait for him by the sea-side. So at last the Mastermaid was forced to let him have his way. But she said,

"Now, when you get home, don't stop so much as to say good day to anyone, but go straight to the stable, and harness the horses, and drive back as quick as you can. Your brothers and sisters and all your friends will come about you. But do as though you did not see them. And above all things, mind you do not taste a morsel of food, for if you do, we shall both come to grief."

All this the Prince promised; but he thought all the time there was little fear of his forgetting her.

Now, just as he came home to the palace, one of his brothers was thinking of holding his bridal feast, and the bride, and all her kith and kin, were just come to the palace. So they all thronged around him, and asked about this thing and that, and wanted him to go in with them. But he made as though he did not see them, and went straight to the stall and got out the horses, and began to put them to. And when they saw they could not get him to go in, they came out to him with meat and drink, and the best of everything they had got ready for the feast; but the Prince would not taste so much as a crumb, and harnessed the horses as fast as he could. At last the bride's sister rolled an apple across the yard to him, saying,

"Well, if you won't eat anything else, you may as well take a bite of this, for you must be both hungry and thirsty after so long a journey."

So he took up the apple and bit a piece out of it; but he had scarcely done so, before he forgot the Mastermaid, and how he was to drive back for her.

"Well, I think I must be mad," he said; "what am I to do with this coach and horses?"

So he put the horses up again, and went along with the others into the palace, and it was soon settled that he should have the bride's sister, the one who had rolled the apple over to him.

There sat the Mastermaid by the seashore, waiting and waiting for the Prince; but no Prince came. At last she went up from the shore, and after she had gone a bit she came to a little hut which stood by itself in a copse close by the king's palace. She went in and asked if she might lodge there. It was an old dame that owned the hut, a cross-grained scolding hag she was as ever you could see. At first she would not hear of the Mastermaid's lodging in her house, but at last, for fair words and high rent, the Mastermaid got leave to be there.

Now the hut was as dark and dirty as a pigsty, so the Mastermaid said she would smarten it up a little, that their house, inside, might look like other people's. The old hag did not like this either, and showed her teeth, and was cross; but the Mastermaid did not mind her. She took her chest of gold, and threw a handful or so into the fire, and lo! the gold melted, and bubbled and boiled over out of the grate, and spread itself over the whole hut, till it was gilded both outside and in. But as soon as the gold began to bubble and boil, the old hag became so frightened that she tried to run out as if the Evil One were at her heels. As she ran out at the door, she forgot to stoop, and gave her head such a knock against the lintel, that she broke her neck, and that was the end of her.

Next morning the Constable passed that way, and you may fancy he could scarce believe his eyes when he saw the golden hut shining and glistening in the copse. But he was still more astonished when he went in and saw the lovely maiden who sat there. To make a long story short, he fell head over heels in love with her, and begged and prayed her to become his wife.

"Well, but have you much money?" asked the Mastermaid.

Yes, for that matter, he said, he was not so badly off, and off he went home to fetch the money, and when he came back at even he brought a half-bushel sack, and set it down on the bench. So the

Mastermaid said she would have him, since he was so rich. But they were scarcely in bed before she said she must get up again,

"For I have forgotten to bank the fire."

"Pray, don't stir out of bed," said the Constable; "I'll see to it."

So he jumped out of bed, and stood on the hearth in a trice.

"As soon as you have got hold of the shovel, just tell me," said the Mastermaid.

"Well, I am holding it now," said the Constable.

Then the Mastermaid said,

"God grant that you may hold the shovel, and the shovel, you, and may you heap hot burning coals over yourself till morning breaks."

So there stood the Constable all night long, shoveling hot burning coals over himself; and though he begged, and prayed, and wept, the coals were not a bit colder for that. As soon as day broke, and he had the power to cast away the shovel, he did not stay long, as you may fancy, but set off as if the Evil One or the bailiff were at his heels; and all who met him stared their eyes out at him, for he cut capers as though he were mad. He could not have looked in worse plight if he had been flayed and tanned, and everyone wondered what had befallen him. But he told no one where he had been, for shame's sake.

Next day the Attorney passed by the place where the Mastermaid lived, and he too saw how it shone and glistened in the copse; so he turned aside to find out who owned the hut. When he came in and saw the lovely maiden, he fell more in love with her than had the Constable, and began to woo her in hot haste.

Well, the Mastermaid asked him, as she had asked the Constable, if he had a good lot of money. The Attorney said he wasn't so badly off; and as a proof he went home to fetch his money. So at even he came back with a great fat sack or money—I think it was a whole bushel sack—and set it down on the bench; and the long and the short of the matter was, that she consented to have him, and they went to bed. But all at once the Mastermaid said she had forgotten to shut the door of the porch, and that she must get up and make it fast for the night.

"What, you to do that!" said the Attorney, "while I lie here? That can never be; lie still, while I go and do it."

So up he jumped, like a pea on a drumhead, and ran out into the porch.

"Tell me," said the Mastermaid, "when you have hold of the door latch."

"I've got hold of it now," said the Attorney.

"God grant, then," said the Mastermaid, "that you may hold the door, and the door, you, and that you may go from wall to wall till day dawns."

So you may fancy what a dance the Attorney had all night long; such a waltz he never had before, and I don't think he would much care if he never had such a waltz again. Now he pulled the door forward, and then the door pulled him back, and so he went on, now dashed into one corner of the porch, and now into the other, till he was almost battered to death. At first he began to curse and swear, and then to beg and pray, but the door cared for nothing but holding its own till break of day. As soon as it let go its hold, off set the Attorney, leaving behind him his money to pay for his night's lodging, and forgetting his courtship altogether, for to tell the truth, he was afraid lest the house-door should come dancing after him. All who met him stared and gaped at him, for he too cut capers like a madman, and he could not have looked in worse plight if he had spent the whole night in butting against a flock of rams.

The third day the Sheriff passed that way, and he too saw the golden hut, and turned aside to find out who lived there; and he had scarce set eyes on the Mastermaid, before he began to woo her. So she answered him as she had answered the other two. If he had lots of money she would have him, if not, he might go about his business. Well, the Sheriff said he wasn't so badly off, and he would go home and fetch the money. When he came again at even, he had a bigger sack even than that of the Attorney—it must have been at least a bushel and a half—which he put down on the bench. So it was soon settled that he was to have the Mastermaid. But they had scarcely gone to bed before the Mastermaid said she had forgotten to bring home the calf from the meadow, so she must get up and drive him into the stall. Then the Sheriff swore by all the powers that that should never be, and, stout and fat as he was, up he jumped as nimbly as a kitten.

"Well, only tell me when you've got hold of the calf's tail," said the Mastermaid.

"Now I have hold of it," said the Sheriff.

"God grant," said the Mastermaid, "that you may hold the calf's tail, and the calf's tail, you, and that you may make a tour of the world together till day dawns."

Well you may just fancy how the Sheriff had to stretch his legs. Away they went, the calf and he, high and low, across hill and dale, and the more the Sheriff cursed and swore, the faster the calf ran and jumped. At dawn of day the poor Sheriff was well nigh broken-winded, and so glad was he to let go the calf's tail, that he forgot his sack of money and everything else. As he was a great man, he went a little slower than the Attorney and the Constable, but the slower he went the more time people had to gape and stare at him; and I must say they made good use of their time, for he was terribly tattered and torn, after his dance with the calf.

THE next day was fixed for the wedding at the palace. The eldest brother was to drive to church with his bride, and the younger, who had lived with the Giant, with the bride's sister. But when they had got into the coach, and were just going to drive off, one of the trace pins snapped off; and though they made at least three in its place, they all broke, from whatever sort of wood they were made. So time went on and on, and they couldn't get to church, and everyone grew very downcast. But all at once the Constable—for he too was bidden to the wedding—said that yonder away in the copse lived a maiden.

"And if you can only get her to lend you the handle of her shovel with which she makes up her fire, I know very well that it will hold."

Well! they sent a messenger on the spot, with such a pretty message to the maiden, to know if they couldn't borrow her shovel which the Constable had spoken of. The maiden said yes, they might have it; so they got a trace pin which wasn't likely to snap.

But all at once, just as they were driving off, the bottom of the coach tumbled to bits. So they set to work to make a new bottom as they best might. But it mattered not how many nails they put into it, nor of what wood they made it, for as soon as ever they got the bottom well into the coach and were driving off, snap it went in two again, and they were even worse off than when they had lost the trace pin. Just then the Attorney said—for if the Constable was there, you may fancy the Attorney was there too—"Away yonder, in the copse, lives a maiden, and if you could only get her to lend you one-half of her porch door, I know it can hold together."

Well! they sent another messenger to the copse, and asked so prettily if they couldn't borrow the gilded porch door which the Attorney had talked of that they got it on the spot. So now they were ready to set out. But, alas, the horses were not strong enough to draw the coach, though there were six of them! They hitched on eight, then ten, and twelve, but the more they put on, and the more the coachman whipped, the coach still wouldn't stir an inch. By this time it was far on into the day, and everyone about the palace was in doleful dumps; for to church they must go. And yet it looked as if they would never get there. So at last the Sheriff said, that yonder in the gilded hut, in the copse, lived a maiden, and if they could only borrow her calf,

"I know it can drag the coach, though it were as heavy as a mountain."

Well they all thought it would look silly to be drawn to church by a calf, but there was no help for it. So they had to send a third time, and ask prettily, in the King's name, if they couldn't get the loan of the calf the Sheriff had spoken of. The Mastermaid let them have it on the spot, for she was not going to say no this time either. So they harnessed the calf in front of it to see if it would do any good. Away went the coach over hill and dale, and stock and stone, so that they could scarce draw their breath. Sometimes they were on the ground, and sometimes up in the air, and when they reached the church, the calf began to run round and round it like a spinning jenny, so that they had hard work to get out of the coach, and into the church. When they went back, it was the same story, only they went faster, and they reached the palace almost before they knew they had set out.

Now when they sat down to dinner, the Prince who had served with the Giant said he thought they ought to ask the maiden who had lent them her shovel handle and porch door, and calf, to come up to the palace.

"For," said he, "if we hadn't got these three things, we should have been sticking here still."

Yes; the King thought that only fair and right, so he sent five of his best men down to the gilded hut to greet the maiden from the

King, and to ask her if she would be so good as to come up and dine at the palace.

"Greet the King from me," said the Mastermaid, "and tell him, if he's too good to come to me, so am I too good to go to him."

So the King himself had to go, and then the Mastermaid went up with him without more ado; and as the King thought she was not what she seemed to be, he sat her down in the highest seat by the side of the youngest bridegroom.

Now, when they had sat a little while at table, the Mastermaid took out her golden apple, and the golden cock and hen, which she had carried off from the Giant, and put them down on the table before her, and the cock and hen began at once to peck at one another, and to fight for the golden apple.

"Oh! only look," said the Prince; "see how those two strive for the apple."

"Yes!" said the Mastermaid; "so we two strove to get away that time when we were together on the hillside."

Then the spell was broken, and the Prince knew her again, and you may fancy how glad he was. But as for the bride's sister who was a witch and who had rolled the apple over to him, he had her torn to pieces between twenty-four horses, so that there was not a bit of her left. After that they went on with the wedding in real earnest, and though they were still stiff and footsore, the Constable, the Attorney, and the Sheriff, kept it up with the best of them.

SORIA MORIA CASTLE

* * *

ONCE on a time there was a poor couple who had a son whose name was Halvor. Ever since he was a little boy he would turn his hand to nothing, but just sat and groped about in the ashes. His father and mother often put him out to learn this trade or that, but Halvor could stay nowhere; for, when he had been there a day or two, he would run away from his master, and never stop till he was sitting again in the ingle, poking about in the cinders.

Well, one day a skipper came and asked Halvor if he hadn't a mind to go with him to sea, and see strange lands. Yes, Halvor would like that very much; so he wasn't long in getting himself ready.

How long they sailed I'm sure I can't tell; but the end of it was, they ran into a great storm, and when it had blown over, and the sea was calm again, they couldn't tell where they were; for they had been driven away to a strange coast, which none of them knew anything about.

As there was just no wind at all, they stayed lying wind-bound there, and Halvor asked the skipper's leave to go on shore and look about him; he would sooner go, he said, than lie there and sleep.

"Do you think you're fit to show yourself before folk?" said the skipper. "Why, you've no clothes than those rags you stand in!"

But Halvor stuck to his own plan, and so at last he got leave, but he was to be sure to come back as soon as ever it began to blow. So off he went and found a lovely land for wherever he went there were fine large flat cornfields and rich meads, though he couldn't catch a glimpse of a living soul. Well, it began to blow, but Halvor, who thought he hadn't seen enough yet, wanted to walk a little farther just to see if he couldn't meet any folk. After a while he came to a broad high road, so smooth and even, you might easily roll an egg along it. Halvor followed this, and when evening drew on he saw a great castle ever so far off, from which the sunbeams shone. As he had now walked the whole day and hadn't taken a bit to eat with him, he was as hungry as a hunter; but still, the nearer he came to the castle, the more afraid he got.

In the castle kitchen a great fire was blazing, so Halvor went into it. Such a kitchen he had never seen in all his born days; it was so grand and fine. There were vessels of silver and vessels of gold—but never a living soul. So when Halvor had stood there a while and still no one came he went and opened a door, and there, inside, sat a Princess who spun upon a spinning wheel.

"Nay, nay, now!" she called out; "dare Christian folk come hither? But you'd best be off about your business, if you don't want the troll to gobble you up; for here lives a troll with three heads."

"All one to me," said the lad. "I'd be just as glad to hear he had four heads. Besides, I'd like to see what kind of fellow he is. As for going, I won't go. I've done no harm. But meat you must get me, for I'm almost starved to death."

When Halvor had eaten his fill, the Princess told him to try if he could brandish the sword that hung against the wall. No, he couldn't brandish it, he couldn't even lift it.

"Oh!" said the Princess. "Go and take a pull of that flask that hangs by its side; that's what the troll does every time he goes out to use the sword."

So Halvor took a pull, and in the twinkling of an eye he could brandish the sword like nothing; and now he thought it high time that the troll came back. Lo! just then up came the troll puffing and blowing. Halvor jumped behind the door.

"Hutetu," said the troll, as he put his head in at the door. "What a smell of Christian man's blood!"

"Aye," said Halvor, "you'll soon know that to your cost," and with that he hewed off all his heads.

The Princess was so glad that she was free, she both danced and sang. Then all at once she called her sisters to mind, and so she said,

"Would my sisters were free too!"

"Where are they?" asked Halvor.

Well, she told him all about it; one was taken away by a troll to his castle which lay fifty miles off, and the other, by another troll to his castle which was fifty miles further still.

"But now," she said, "you must first help me get this ugly carcass out of the house."

Yes, Halvor was so strong, he swept everything away, and made it all clean and tidy in no time. So they had a good and happy time of it, and next morning he set off at peep of gray dawn. He could take no rest by the way, but ran and walked the whole day. When he first saw the castle he was a little afraid, for it was far grander than the first. But here too there wasn't a living soul to be seen, so Halvor went into the kitchen. He didn't stop there, but went straight on into the house.

"Nay, nay," called out the Princess. "Dare Christian folk come hither? I don't know I'm sure, how long it is since I came here, but in all that time I haven't seen a Christian man. 'Twere best you saw how to get away as fast as you came; for here lives a troll, who has six heads."

"I wouldn't go," said Halvor, "if he had six heads besides."

"He'll take you up and swallow you down alive," said the Princess.

But it was no good, Halvor wouldn't go; he wasn't at all afraid of the troll, but meat and drink he must have, for he was half starved after his long journey. Well, when he had got as much food as he wished, the Princess wanted him to be off again.

"No," said Halvor, "I won't go. I've done no harm, and I've nothing to be afraid of."

"He won't stay to ask that," said the Princess, "for he'll take you without law or leave. But as you won't go, just try if you can brandish that sword yonder, which the troll wields in war."

He couldn't brandish it, and then the Princess said he must take a pull at the flask which hung by its side; and when he had done that he could brandish it.

Just then back came the troll. He was both stout and big, so big that he had to go sideways to get through the door. When the troll got his first head in he called out,

"Hutetu, what a smell of Christian man's blood!"

But at that very moment Halvor hewed off his first head, and so on with all the rest as they popped in. The Princess was overjoyed, but just then she came to think of her sisters, and wished out loud that they too, might be free. Halvor thought that might easily be done, and wanted to be off at once, but as he first had to help the Princess get the troll's carcass out of the way, he could only set out the next morning.

It was a long way to the castle, and he had to walk fast and run hard to reach it in time, but about nightfall he saw the castle, which was far finer and grander than either of the others. This time he wasn't the least bit afraid, but walked straight through the kitchen, and into the castle. There sat a Princess who was so pretty, there was no end to her loveliness. She too, like the others, told him there hadn't been Christian folk there since she had come thither, and bade him go away again, else the troll would swallow him alive, adding that he had nine heads.

"Aye, aye," said Halvor, "if he had nine other heads, and nine others still, I won't go away," and so he stood fast before the stove. Though the Princess kept on begging him so prettily to go away, lest the troll should gobble him up, Halvor said,

"Let him come as soon as he likes."

So she gave him the troll's sword, and bade him take a pull at the flask, that he might be able to brandish and wield it.

Just then back came the troll, puffing and blowing and tearing along. He was far stouter and bigger than the other two, and he too had to turn sideways to get through the door. So when he got his first head in, he said as the others had said,

"HUTETU, what a smell of Christian man's blood!"

That very moment Halvor hewed off the first head and then all the rest. But the last was the toughest of them all, and it was the hardest bit of work Halvor had to do to get it hewn off, although he knew very well he had strength enough to do it.

So all the Princesses came together to that castle, which was called Soria Moria Castle, and they were glad and happy as they had never been in all their lives before. They all were fond of Halvor and

Halvor of them, and he might choose the one he liked best for his bride; but the youngest was fondest of him of all the three.

But after a while, Halvor went about, so strange and dull and silent, that the Princesses asked him what he lacked, and if he didn't like living with them any longer? Yes, he did, for they had enough and to spare, and he was well off in every way, but still somehow or other, he did so long to go home, for his father and mother were alive and he had such a great wish to see them.

Well, they thought that might be done easily enough.

"You shall go thither and come back hither, safe and unscathed, if you will only follow our advice," said the Princesses.

Yes, he'd be sure to mind all they said. So they dressed him up till he was as grand as a king's son, and they set a ring on his finger, and that was such a ring, he could wish himself thither and hither with it. But they told him to be sure not to take it off, and not to name their names, for if he did so, there would be an end of all his luck, and he'd never see them any more.

"If I only stood at home I'd be glad," said Halvor; and it was done as he had wished. Then stood Halvor at his father's cottage door before he knew a thing about it. Now it was about dusk at even, and so, when they saw such a grand stately lord walk in, the old couple got so afraid they began to bow and scrape. Then Halvor asked if he might stay there, and lodge there that night. No; that he couldn't.

"We can't do it at all," they said, "for we haven't this thing or that thing which such a lord is used to have. 'Twere best your lordship went up to the farm, not a long way off—for you can see the chimneys—and there they have lots of everything."

Halvor wouldn't hear of it—he wanted to stop. But the old couple stuck to their own, that he had better go to the farmer's; there he would get both meat and drink. As for them, they hadn't even a chair to offer him to sit down on.

"No," said Halvor, "I won't go up there till tomorrow early. But let me just stay here tonight; if the worst comes to the worst, I can sit in the chimney corner."

Well, they couldn't say anything against that; so Halvor sat down by the ingle, and began to poke about in the ashes, just as he used to do when he lay at home in the old days, and stretched his lazy bones.

They chattered and talked about many things, and they told Halvor about this thing and that; and so he asked them if they had never had any children.

Yes, yes, they had once a lad whose name was Halvor, but they didn't know whether he were dead or alive.

"Couldn't it be me, now?" said Halvor.

"Let me see; I could tell him well enough," said the old wife, and rose up. "Our Halvor was so lazy and dull, he never did a thing; and besides, he was so ragged, that one tatter took hold of the next tatter on him. No; there never was the making of such a fine fellow in him as you are, master."

A little while after, the old wife went to the hearth to poke up the fire, and when the blaze fell on Halvor's face, just as when he was at home of old poking about in the ashes, she knew him at once.

"Ah! but is it you after all, Halvor?" she cried. And then there was such joy for the old couple, there was no end to it. He was forced to tell how he had fared, and the old dame was so fond and proud of him, nothing would do but he must go up at once to the farmer's, and show himself to the girls, who had always looked down on him. And off she went first, and Halvor followed after. So, when she got up there, she told them all how her Halvor had come home again, and they should just see how grand he was, for, said she, "he looks like nothing but a king's son."

"All very fine," said the girls, and tossed their heads. "We'll be bound he's just the same beggarly ragged boy he always was."

Just then in walked Halvor, and then the girls were all so taken aback, they forgot their sarks in the ingle, where they were sitting darning their clothes, and ran out in their smocks. Well, when they were got back again, they were so shamefaced they scarce dared look at Halvor, towards whom they had always been proud and haughty.

"Aye, aye," said Halvor, "you always thought yourselves so pretty and neat, no one could come near you; but now you should just see the eldest Princess I have set free; against her you look just like milkmaids; and the midmost is prettier still; but the youngest, who is my sweetheart, she's fairer than both sun and moon. Would to Heaven she were only here," said Halvor, "then you'd see what you would see."

He had scarce uttered these words before there they stood; but then he felt so sorry, for now what they had said came into his mind. Up at the farm there was a great feast got ready for the Princesses, and much was made of them, but they wouldn't stop there.

"No; we want to go down to your father and mother," they said to Halvor; "and so we'll go out now and look about us."

So he went down with them, and they came to a great lake just outside the farm. Close by the water was a lovely green bank. Here the Princesses said they would sit and rest a while; they thought it so sweet to sit down and look over the water.

So they sat down there, and when they had sat a while, the youngest Princess said,

"I may as well comb your hair a little, Halvor."

Yes, Halvor laid his head on her lap, and so she combed his bonny locks, and it wasn't long before Halvor fell fast asleep. Then she took the ring from his finger, and put another in its stead; and then she said,

"Now hold me all together! and now, would we were all in Soria Moria Castle."

So when Halvor woke up, he could very well tell that he had lost the Princesses, and began to weep and wail; and he was so downcast, they couldn't comfort him at all. In spite of all his father and mother said, he wouldn't stop there, but took farewell of them, and said he was sure not to see them again; for if he couldn't find the Princesses again, he thought it not worth while to live.

Well, he had still three hundred dollars left, so he put them into his pocket, and set out on his way. So, when he had walked a while, he met a man with a tidy horse, and he wanted to buy it, and began to chaffer with the man.

"Aye," said the man, "to tell the truth, I never thought of selling him; but if we could strike a bargain, perhaps—"

"What do you want for him," asked Halvor.

"I didn't give much for him, nor is he worth much. He's a brave horse to ride, but he can't draw at all. Still, he's strong enough to carry your knapsack and you too, turn and turn about," said the man.

At last they agreed on the price, and Halvor laid the knapsack on him, and so he walked a bit, and rode a bit, turn and turn about. At night he came to a green plain where stood a great tree, at the roots of which he sat down. There he let the horse loose, but he didn't lie down to sleep, but opened his knapsack and took a meal. At peep of day off he set again, for he could take no rest. So he rode and walked and walked and rode the whole day through the wide wood, where there were so many green spots and glades that shone so bright and lovely between the trees. He didn't know at all where he was or whither he was going, but he gave himself no more time to rest, than when his horse cropped a bit of grass, and he took a snack out of his knapsack when they came to one of those green glades. So he went on walking and riding by turns, and as for the wood there seemed to be no end to it.

But at dusk the next day he saw a light gleaming away through the trees.

"Would there were folk hereaway," thought Halvor, "that I might warm myself a bit and get a morsel to keep body and soul together."

When he got up to it, he saw the light came from a wretched little hut, and through the window he saw an old, old couple inside. They were as grey-headed as a pair of doves, and the old wife had such a nose! Why, it was so long she used it for a poker to stir the fire as she sat in the ingle.

"Good evening," said Halvor.

"Good evening," said the old wife.

"But what errand can you have in coming hither?" she went on. "For no Christian folk have been here these hundred years and more."

Well, Halvor told her all about himself, and how he wanted to get to Soria Moria Castle, and asked if she knew the way thither.

"No," said the old wife, "that I don't; but see now, here comes the Moon. I'll ask her, she'll know all about it, for doesn't she shine on everything?"

So when the Moon stood clear and bright over the tree-tops, the old wife went out.

"Thou Moon, thou Moon," she screamed, "canst thou tell me the way to Soria Moria Castle?"

"No," said the Moon, "that I can't, for the last time I shone there a cloud stood before me."

"Wait a bit still," said the old wife to Halvor. "By and by comes the West Wind; he's sure to know it, for he puffs and blows round every corner."

"Nay, nay," said the old wife when she went out again, "you don't mean to say you've got a horse too; just turn the poor beastie loose in our town, and don't let him stand there and starve to death at the door."

Then she ran on,

"But won't you trade him away to me. We've got an old pair of boots here, with which you can take twenty miles at each stride. Those you shall have for your horse, and so you'll get all the sooner to Soria Moria Castle."

That Halvor was willing to do at once; and the old wife was so glad to have the horse, she was ready to dance and skip for joy.

"For now," she said, "I shall be able to ride to church. I too, think of that."

As for Halvor, he had no rest, and wanted to be off at once, but the old wife said there was no hurry.

"Lie down on the bench and sleep a bit, for we've no bed to offer you, and I'll watch and wake you when the West Wind comes."

So after a while up came the West Wind, roaring and howling along till the walls creaked and groaned again.

Out ran the old wife.

"Thou West Wind, thou West Wind! Canst thou tell me the way to Soria Moria Castle? Here's one who wants to get thither."

"Yes, I know it very well," said the West Wind, "and now I'm just off thither to dry clothes for the wedding that's to be. If he's swift of foot he can go along with me."

Out ran Halvor.

"You'll have to stretch your legs if you mean to keep up," said the West Wind.

So off he set over field and hedge, and hill and fell, and Halvor had hard work to keep up.

"Well," said the West Wind, "now I've no time to stay with you any longer, for I've got to go away yonder and tear down a strip of spruce wood first before I go to the bleaching-ground to dry

the clothes; but if you go alongside the hill you'll come to a lot of women standing washing clothes, and then you've not far to go to Soria Moria Castle."

In a little while Halvor came upon the women who stood washing, and they asked if he had seen anything of the West Wind who was to come and dry the clothes for the wedding.

"Aye, aye, that I have," said Halvor. "He's only gone to tear down a strip of spruce wood. It'll not be long before he's here," and then he asked them the way to Soria Moria Castle.

So they put him into the right way, and when he got to the Castle, the courtyard was full of folk and horses—so full it made one giddy to look at them. But Halvor was so ragged and torn from having followed the West Wind through bush and brier and bog, that he kept to one side, and wouldn't show himself till the last day when the bridal feast was to be.

So when all were to drink the bride and bridegroom's health and wish them luck, as was then right and fitting, and when the cupbearer was to drink to them all again, both knights and squires, last of all he came in turn to Halvor. He drank their health, but let the ring which the Princess had put upon his finger as he lay by the lake, fall into the glass, and bade the cupbearer greet the bride and hand her the glass.

Then up rose the Princess from the board at once.

"Who is most worthy to have one of us," she said, "he that has set us free, or he that here sits by me as bridegroom?"

Well they all said there could be but one voice and will as to that, and when Halvor heard that, he wasn't long in throwing off his beggar's rags, and arraying himself as bridegroom.

"Aye, aye, here is the right one after all," said the youngest Princess as soon as she saw him, and so she sent the other away, and held her wedding with Halvor.

THE SEVEN FOALS

* ** ** *

ONCE on a time there was a poor couple who lived in a wretched hut, far far away in the wood. How they lived I can't tell, but I'm sure it was from hand to mouth, and hard work even then; for they had three sons, and the youngest of them was the Ashlad, of course, for he did little else than lie there and poke about in the ashes.

One day the eldest lad said he would go out to earn his bread, and he soon got leave, and wandered out into the world. There he walked and walked the whole day, and when evening drew in, he came to a king's manor. And there stood the King out on the steps, who asked whither he was bound.

"Oh, I'm going about, looking for a place," said the lad.

"Will you serve me," asked the King, "and watch my seven foals? If you can watch them one whole day, and tell me at night what they eat and what they drink, you shall have the Princess to wife, and half my kingdom; but if you can't, I'll cut three red stripes out of your back. Do you hear?"

Yes! that was an easy task, the lad thought; he'd do that fast enough, never fear.

So next morning, as soon as the first peep of dawn came, the King's coachman let out the seven foals. Away they went, and the lad after them. You may fancy how they tore over hill and dale, through bush and bog. When the lad had run a long time, he began to get weary, and when he had held on a while longer, he had more than enough of his watching. Just then he came to a cleft in a rock, where an old hag sat and spun with a distaff. As soon as she saw the lad who was running after the foals till the sweat ran down his brow, this old hag bawled out,

"Come hither, come hither, my pretty son, and let me comb your hair."

Yes! the lad was willing enough; so he sat down in the cleft of the rock with the old hag, and laid his head on her lap, and she combed his hair all day whilst he lay there, and stretched his lazy bones.

So, when evening drew on, the lad wanted to go away.

"I may just as well toddle straight home now," said he, "for it's no use my going back to the King."

"Stop a bit till it's dark," said the old hag, "and when the King's foals will pass by here again, and you can run home with them, and no one will know that you have lain here all day long, instead of watching the foals."

So, when they came, she gave the lad a flask of water and a clod of turf. Those he was to show to the King, and say that that was what his seven foals ate and drank.

"Have you watched true and well the whole day?" asked the King, when the lad came before him in the evening.

"Yes, I should think so," said the lad.

"Then you can tell me what my seven foals eat and drink," said the King.

"Yes!" and so the lad pulled out the flask of water and the clod of turf, which the old hag had given him.

"Here you see their meat, and here you see their drink," said the lad.

But then the King saw plainly enough how he had watched, and he got so wroth, he ordered his men to chase him away home on the spot; but first they were to cut three red stripes out of his back, and rub salt into them. So when the lad got home again, you may fancy what a temper he was in! He'd gone out once to get a place, he said, but he'd never do so again.

Next day the second son said he would go out into the world to try his luck. His father and mother said "No," and bade him look at his brother's back. But the lad wouldn't give in; he held to his own, and at last he got leave to go, and set off. So when he had walked the whole day, he, too, came to the king's manor. There stood the King out on the steps, who asked whither he was bound. When the lad said he was looking about for a place, the King said he might have a place there, and watch his seven foals. But the King laid down the same punishment, and the same reward, as he had set for his brother. Well, the lad was willing enough. He took the place at once with the King, for he thought he'd soon watch the foals, and tell the King what they ate and drank.

So, in the gray of the morning, the coachman let out the seven foals, and off they went again over hill and dale, and the lad after them. But the same thing happened to him as had befallen his brother. When he had run after the foals a long, long time, till he was both warm and weary, he passed by the cleft in a rock, where an old hag sat and spun with a distaff, and she bawled out to the lad,

"Come hither, come hither, my pretty son, and let me comb your hair."

The lad thought that a good offer, so he let the foals run on their way, and sat down in the cleft with the old hag. There he sat, and there he lay, taking his ease, and stretching his lazy bones the whole day.

When the foals came back at nightfall, he too got a flask of water and a clod of turf from the old hag, to show to the King. But when the King asked the lad,

"Can you tell me now, what my seven foals eat and drink?" the lad pulled out the flask and the clod, and said,

"Here you see their meat, and here you see their drink."

The King got wroth again, and ordered his servants to cut three red stripes out of the lad's back, and rub salt in, and chase him home that very minute. And so when the lad got home, he also told how he had fared, and said, he had gone out once to get a place, but he'd never do so any more.

The third day the Ashlad wanted to set out; he had a great mind to try and watch the seven foals, he said. The others laughed at him, and made game of him, saying,

"When we fared so ill, you'll do it better! A fine joke! You look like it, you, who have never done anything but lie there and poke about in the ashes."

"Yes!" said the Ashlad, "I don't see why I shouldn't go, for I've got it into my head, and can't get it out again."

And so, in spite of all the jeers of the others and the prayers of the old people, there was no help for it, and the Ashlad set out.

After he had walked the whole day, he too came at dusk to the King's manor. There stood the King on the steps, who asked whither he was bound.

"Oh," said the Ashlad, "I'm going about seeing if I can hear of a place."

"Whence do you come then?" said the King, for he wanted to know a little more about him before he took any one into his service.

So the Ashlad said whence he came, and how he was brother to those two who had watched the King's seven foals, and ended by asking if he might try to watch them next day.

"Oh, stuff!" said the King, for he got quite cross if he even thought of them. "If you are brother to those two, you're not worth much, I'll be bound. I've had enough of such scamps."

"Well," said the Ashlad, "since I've come so far, I, too, may just as well get leave to try."

"Oh, very well, with all my heart," said the King. "If you will have your back flayed, you're quite welcome."

"I'd much rather have the Princess," said the Ashlad.

So next morning, at gray of dawn, the coachman let out the seven foals again, and away they went over hill and dale, through bush and bog, and the Ashlad behind them. And so, when he, too, had run a long while, he came to the cleft in the rock, where the old hag sat, spinning at her distaff. She bawled out to the Ashlad,

"Come hither, come hither, my pretty son, and let me comb your hair."

"Don't you wish you might catch me?" said the Ashlad. "Don't you wish you might catch me?" he shouted, as he ran along, leaping and jumping, and holding on by one of the foals' tails. And when he had got well past the cleft in the rock, the youngest foal said,

"Jump upon my back, my lad, for we've a long way before us still."

So the Ashlad jumped up on his back.

They went on, and on, a long, long way.

"Do you see anything now?" said the foal.

"No," said the Ashlad.

They went on a good bit farther.

"Do you see anything now?" asked the foal.

"Oh, no," said the lad.

So when they had gone a great, great way farther—I'm sure I can't tell how far,—the foal asked again,

"Do you see anything now?"

"Yes," said the Ashlad; "now I see something that looks white— just like a tall, big birch trunk."

"Yes," said the foal; "we're going into that trunk."

So when they got to the trunk, the eldest foal took and pushed it to one side, and they saw a door where it had stood, and inside the door was a little room. And in the room there was scarce anything but a little fireplace and one or two benches. But behind the door hung a great rusty sword and a little pitcher. "Can you brandish the sword?" said the foals. "Try."

So the Ashlad tried, but he couldn't. Then they made him take a pull at the pitcher, first once, then twice, and then thrice, and then he could wield it easily.

"Yes," said the foals, "now you may take the sword with you, and with it you must cut off all our seven heads on your wedding day. Then we'll be princes again as we were before. For we are brothers

of that Princess whom you are to have when you can tell the King what we eat and drink. But an ugly troll has thrown this shape over us. Now mind, when you have hewn off our heads, take care to lay each head at the tail of the trunk which it belonged to before, and then the spell will have no more power over us."

Yes! The Ashlad promised all that, and then on they went.

And when they had travelled a long, long way, the foal asked,

"Do you see anything?"

"No," said the Ashlad.

So they travelled many, many miles again, over hill and dale.

"Now then," said the foal, "do you see anything now?"

"I see something that glitters," said the Ashlad.

"Yes," said the foal, "that's a river we've got to cross."

Over the river was a long, grand bridge; and when they had got over to the other side, they travelled on a long, long way. At last the foal asked again, if the Ashlad didn't see anything.

Yes, this time he saw something that looked black, far in the distance, just as though it were a church steeple.

"Yes," said the foal, "that's where we're going to turn in."

So when the foals got into the churchyard, they became men again, and looked like Princes, with such fine clothes that it glistened from them. So they went into the church and took the bread and wine from the priest who stood at the altar. And the Ashlad went in too. But when the priest had laid his hands on the Princes, and given them the blessing, they went out of the church again, and the Ashlad went out too; but he took with him a flask of wine and a wafer. And as soon as ever the seven Princes came out into the churchyard, they were turned into foals again, and the Ashlad got up on the back of the youngest, and they all went back the same way that they had come; only they went much, much faster. First they crossed the bridge, next they passed the trunk, and then they passed the old hag, who sat at the cleft and spun. And they went by her so fast, that the Ashlad couldn't hear what the old hag screeched after him; but he heard enough to know she was in an awful rage.

It was almost dark when they got back to the manor, and the King, himself, stood out on the steps and waited for them.

"Have you watched well and true the whole day?" said he to the Ashlad.

"I've done my best," answered the Ashlad.

"Then you can tell me what my seven foals eat and drink," said the King.

Then the Ashlad pulled out the flask of wine and the wafer, and showed them to the King.

"Here you see their meat, and here you see their drink," said he.

"Yes," said the King, "you have watched true and well, and you shall have the Princess and half the kingdom."

So they made ready the wedding feast, and the King said it should be such a grand one, it should be the talk far and near.

But when they sat down to the bridal feast, the bridegroom got up and went down to the stable, for he said he had forgotten something, and must go fetch it. And when he got down there, he did as the foals had said, and hewed their heads off, all seven, the eldest first, and the others after him; and at the same time he took care to lay each head at the tail of the foal to which it belonged. And as he did this, lo! they all became Princes again.

So when he went into the bridal hall with the seven princes, the King was so glad he both kissed the Ashlad and patted him on the back, and his bride was still more glad of him than she had been before.

"Half the kingdom you have got already," said the King, "and the other half you shall have after my death; for my sons can easily get themselves lands and wealth, now they are princes again."

And so, like enough, there was mirth and fun at that wedding. I was there too; but there was no one to care for poor me. And so I got nothing but a bit of bread and butter, and I laid it down on the stove, and the bread was burnt and the butter ran, and so I didn't get even the smallest crumb. Wasn't that a great shame?

DAPPLEGRIM

* ** ** *

ONCE on a time there was a rich couple who had twelve sons; but the youngest, when he was grown up, said he wouldn't stay any longer at home, but be off into the world to try his luck. His father and mother said he did very well at home, and had better stay where he was. But no, he couldn't rest; away he must and would go. So at last they gave him leave. And when he had walked a good bit, he came to a king's palace, where he asked for a place, and got it.

Now the daughter of the King of that land had been carried off into the hill by a troll, and the King had no other children; so he and all his land were in great grief and sorrow, and the King gave his word that anyone who could set her free should have the Princess and half the kingdom. But there was no one who could do it, though many tried.

So when the lad had been there a year or so, he longed to go home again and see his father and mother, and back he went. But when he got home his father and mother were dead, and his brothers had shared all that the old people owned between them, and so there was nothing left for the lad.

"Shan't I have anything at all, then, out of father's and mother's goods?" said the lad.

"Who could tell you were still alive, when you went gadding and wandering about so long?" said his brothers. "But all the same, there are twelve mares up in the mountain pastures which we haven't yet shared among us; if you choose to take them for your share, you're quite welcome."

Yes! the lad was quite content; so he thanked his brothers, and went at once up on the mountain, where the twelve mares were sent to pasture. And when he got up there and found them, each of them had a foal at her side, and one of them had besides, along with her, a big dapple-gray foal, which was so sleek that the sun shone from its coat.

"A fine fellow you are, my little foal," said the lad.

"Yes," said the foal. "But if you'll only kill all the other foals, so that I may run and suck all the mares for one year more, you'll see how big and sleek I'll be then."

Yes! the lad was ready to do that; so he killed all those twelve foals, and went home again.

When he came back the next year to look after his foal and mares, the foal was so fat and sleek, that the sun shone from its coat, and it had grown so big, the lad had hard work to mount it. As for the mares, they had each of them another foal.

"Well, it's quite plain I lost nothing by letting you suck all my twelve mares," said the lad to the yearling. "But now you're big enough to come along with me."

"No," said the colt, "I must bide here a year longer. And now kill all the twelve foals, that I may suck all the mares this year too, and you'll see how big and sleek I'll be by summer."

Yes! the lad did that; and next year when he went up to the pastures to look after his colt and the mares, each mare had her foal, but the dapple colt was so tall the lad couldn't reach up to his crest when he wanted to feel how fat he was; and so sleek he was, too, that his coat glistened in the sunshine.

"Big and beautiful you were last year, my colt," said the lad, "but this year you're far grander. There's no such horse in the King's stable. But now you must come along with me."

"No," said Dapple again, "I must stay here one year more. Kill the twelve foals as before, that I may suck the mares the whole year, and then just come and look at me when the summer comes."

Yes! the lad did that. He killed the foals, and went away home.

But when he went up next year to look after Dapple and the mares, he was quite astonished. So tall, and stout, and sturdy, he never thought a horse could be; for Dapple had to lay down on all fours before the lad could bestride him, and it was hard work to get up even then, although he lay flat. And his coat was so smooth and sleek, the sunbeams shone from it as from a looking-glass.

This time Dapple was willing enough to follow the lad, so he jumped up on his back, and when he came riding home to his brothers, they were dumbfounded, for such a horse they had never heard of nor seen before.

"If you will only get me the best shoes you can for my horse, and the grandest saddle and bridle that are to be found," said the lad, "you may have my twelve mares that graze up on the hill yonder, and their twelve foals into the bargain." For you must know that this year too every mare had her foal.

Yes, his brothers were ready to do that, and so the lad got such strong shoes under his horse, that the stones flew high aloft as he rode away across the hills; and he had a golden saddle and a golden bridle, which gleamed and glistened a long way off.

"Now we're off to the King's palace," said Dapplegrim—that was his name. "But mind you ask the King for a good stable and good fodder for me."

Yes! the lad said he would mind; he'd be sure not to forget.

And when he rode off from his brothers' house, you may be sure it wasn't long, with such a horse under him, before he got to the King's palace.

When he came there the King was standing on the steps, and stared and stared at the man who came riding along.

"Nay, nay!" said he, "such a man and such a horse I never yet saw in all my life."

But when the lad asked if he could get a place in the King's household, the King was so glad he was ready to jump and dance as he stood on the steps.

Well, they said, perhaps he might get a place there.

"Aye," said the lad, "but I must have good stable-room for my horse, and fodder that one can trust."

Yes! he should have meadow-hay and oats, as much as Dapple could cram, and all the other knights had to lead their horses out of the stable that Dapplegrim might stand alone, and have it all to himself.

But it wasn't long before all the others in the King's household began to be jealous of the lad, and there was no end to the bad things they would have done to him, if they had only dared. At last they thought of telling the King he had said he was man enough to set the King's daughter free—whom the troll had long since carried away into the hill—if he only chose. The King called the lad before him, and said he had heard the lad said he was good to do so and so; so now he must go and do it. If he did it, he knew how the King had promised his daughter and half the kingdom, and that promise would be faithfully kept; if he didn't, he should be killed.

The lad kept on saying he never said any such thing; but it was no good—the King wouldn't even listen to him; and so the end of it was he was forced to say he'd go and try.

So he went into the stable, down in the mouth and heavy-hearted, and then Dapplegrim asked him at once why he was in such dumps.

The lad told him all, and how he couldn't tell which way to turn.

"For, as for setting the Princess free, that's downright stuff."

"Oh! but it might be done, perhaps," said Dapplegrim. "I'll help you through; but you must first have me well shod. You must go and ask for ten pounds of iron and twelve pounds of steel for the shoes, and one smith to hammer and another to hold."

Yes, the lad did that, and got yes for answer. He got both the iron and the steel, and so Dapplegrim was shod both strong and well, and off went the lad from the courtyard in a cloud of dust.

But when he came to the hill into which the Princess had been carried, the pinch was how to get up the steep wall of rock where the troll's cave was, in which the Princess had been hid.

For you must know the hill stood straight up and down right on end, as upright as a house wall, and as smooth as a sheet of glass.

The first time the lad went at it he got a little way up; but then Dapple's fore-legs slipped, and down they went again, with a sound like thunder on the hill.

The second time he rode at it he got some way further up; but then one fore-leg slipped, and down they went with a crash like a landslide.

But the third time Dapple said,

"Now we must show our mettle," and went at it again till the stones flew heaven-high about them, and so they got up.

Then the lad rode right into the cave at full speed, and caught up the Princess, and threw her over his saddle-bow, and out and down again before the troll had time even to get on his legs; and so the Princess was freed.

When the lad came back to the palace, the King was both happy and glad to get his daughter back; that you may well believe. But somehow or other, though I don't know how, the others about the court had so brought it about that the King was angry with the lad after all.

"Thanks you shall have for freeing my Princess," said he to the lad, when he brought the Princess into the hall, and greeted the King.

"She ought to be mine as well as yours; for you're a wordfast man, I hope," said the lad.

"Aye, aye!" said the King, "have her you shall, since I said it; but, first of all, you must make the sun shine into my palace hall."

Now, you must know there was a high steep ridge of rock close outside the windows, which threw such a shade over the hall that never a sunbeam shone into it.

"That wasn't in our bargain," answered the lad. "But I see this is past praying against; I must e'en go and try my luck, for the Princess I must and will have."

So down he went to Dapple, and told him what the King wanted, and Dapplegrim thought it might easily be done. But first of all he must be new shod; and for that ten pounds of iron, and twelve pounds of steel besides, were needed, and two smiths, one to hammer and the other to hold, and then they'd soon get the sun to shine into the palace hall.

So when the lad asked for all these things, he got them at once— the King couldn't say nay for very shame. And so Dapplegrim got new shoes, and such shoes! Then the lad jumped up on his back, and off they went again; and for every leap that Dapplegrim gave, down sank the ridge fifteen ells into the earth, and so they went on till there was nothing left of the ridge for the King to see.

When the lad got back to the King's palace, he asked the King if the Princess were not his now; for now no one could say that the sun didn't shine into the hall. But then the others set the King's back up again, and he answered the lad should have her of course, he had never thought of anything else, but first he must get as grand a horse for the bride to ride on to church as the bridegroom had himself.

The lad said the King hadn't spoken a word about this before, and that he thought he had now fairly earned the Princess. But the King held to his own, and more, if the lad couldn't do that he should lose his life; that was what the King said. So the lad went down to the stable in doleful dumps, as you may well fancy, and there he told Dapplegrim all about it—how the King had laid that task on him, to find the bride as good a horse as the bridegroom had himself, else he would lose his life.

"But that's not so easy," he said, "for your match isn't to be found in the wide world."

"Oh, yes, I have a match," said Dapplegrim. "But 'tisn't so easy to find him, for he abides in Hell. Still, we'll try. And now you must go up to the King and ask for new shoes for me—ten pounds of iron, and twelve pounds of steel, and two smiths, one to hammer and one to hold; and mind you see that the points and ends of these shoes are sharp. And twelve sacks full of grain and twelve slaughtered oxen, we must have with us. And mind, we must have the twelve ox-hides, with twelve hundred spikes driven into each; and, let me see, a big tar-barrel. That's all we want."

So the lad went up to the King and asked for all that Dapplegrim had said, and the King again thought he couldn't say nay, for shame's sake, so the lad got all he wanted.

Well, he jumped up on Dapplegrim's back, and rode away from the palace, and when he had ridden far, far over the hill and heath, Dapple asked,

"Do you hear anything?"

"Yes, I hear an awful hissing and rustling up in the air," said the lad, "I think I'm getting afraid."

"That's all the wild birds that fly through the wood. They are sent to stop us. But just cut a hole in the corn-sacks, and then they'll have so much to do with the corn, they'll forget us quite."

The lad did that; he cut holes in the corn-sacks, so that the rye and barley ran out on all sides. Then all the wild birds that were in the wood came flying round them so thick that the sunbeams grew dark. But as soon as they saw the corn, they couldn't keep to their purpose, but flew down and began to pick and scratch at the rye and barley, and after that they began to fight among themselves. As for Dapplegrim and the lad, they forgot all about them, and did them no harm. So the lad rode on and on—far, far over mountain and dale, over sandhills and moor. Then Dapplegrim began to prick up his ears again, and at last he asked the lad if he heard anything.

"Yes! now I hear such an ugly roaring and howling in the wood all round, it makes me quite afraid."

"Ah!" said Dapplegrim, "that's all the wild beasts that range through the wood, and they're sent out to stop us. But just cast out the twelve carcasses of the oxen, that will give them enough to do, and so they'll forget us outright."

Yes! the lad cast out the carcasses, and then all the wild beasts in the wood, both bears, and wolves, and lions—all fell beasts of all kinds—came after them. But when they saw the carcasses, they began to fight for them among themselves, till blood flowed in streams; but Dapplegrim and the lad they quite forgot.

So the lad rode far away, through many a country for Dapplegrim didn't let the grass grow under him, as you may fancy. At last Dapple gave a great neigh.

"Do you hear anything?" he said.

"Yes, I hear something like a colt neighing loud, a long, long way off," answered the lad.

"That's a full-grown colt then," said Dapplegrim, "if we hear him neigh so loud such a long way off."

After that they travelled a good bit, through some more countries. Then Dapplegrim gave another neigh.

"Now listen, and tell me if you hear anything," he said.

"Yes, now I hear a neigh like a full-grown horse," answered the lad.

"Aye! aye!" said Dapplegrim. "You'll hear him once again, soon, and then you'll hear he's got a voice of his own."

So they travelled on and on through countries still farther away. And then Dapplegrim neighed the third time; but before he could ask the lad if he heard anything, something gave such a neigh across the heathy hillside, the lad thought hill and rock would surely be rent asunder.

"Now, he's here!" said Dapplegrim. "Make haste, now, and throw the ox hides, with the spikes in them, over me, and throw down the tar-barrel on the plain; then climb up into that great spruce-fir yonder. When it comes, fire will flash out of both nostrils, and then the tar-barrel will catch fire. Now, mind what I say. If the flame rises, I win; if it falls, I lose. But if you see me winning take and cast the bridle—you must take it off me—over its head, and then it will be tame enough."

So just as the lad had done throwing the ox hides, with the spikes, over Dapplegrim, and had cast down the tar-barrel on the plain, and had got well up into the spruce-fir, up galloped a horse, with fire flashing out of his nostrils, and the flame caught the tar-barrel at once. Then Dapplegrim and the strange horse began to fight till the stones flew heaven high. They fought, and bit, and kicked, both with fore feet and hind feet, and sometimes the lad could see them, and sometimes he couldn't; but at last the flame began to rise; for wherever the strange horse kicked or bit, he met the spiked hides, and at last he had to yield. When the lad saw that, he wasn't long in getting down from the tree, and in throwing the bridle over its head, and then it was so tame you could hold it with a pack-thread.

And that horse was dappled too, and so like Dapplegrim, you could not tell which was which. Then the lad bestrode the new Dapple he had broken, and rode home to the palace, and old Dapplegrim ran loose by his side. So when he got home, there stood the King out in the yard.

"Can you tell me now," said the lad, "which is the horse I have caught and broken, and which is the one I had before? If you can't I think your daughter is fairly mine."

Then the King went and looked at both Dapples, high and low, before and behind, but there wasn't a hair on one which wasn't on the other as well.

"No," said the King, "that I can't. And since you've got my daughter such a grand horse for her wedding, you shall have her with all my heart. But still we'll have one trial more, just to see whether you're fated to have her. First, she shall hide herself twice, and then you shall hide yourself twice. If you can find out her hiding place, and she can't find out yours, why then, you're fated to have her, and so you shall have her."

"That's not in the bargain, either," said the lad. "But we must just try, since it must be so." And so the Princess went off to hide herself first.

She turned herself into a duck, and lay swimming on a pond that was close to the palace. But the lad only ran down to the stable, and asked Dapplegrim what she had done with herself.

"Oh, you only need to take your gun," said Dapplegrim, "and go down to the brink of the pond, and aim at the duck which lies swimming about there, and she'll soon show herself."

So the lad snatched up his gun and ran off to the pond. "I'll just take a pop at this duck," he said and began to aim at it.

"Nay, nay, dear friend, don't shoot. It's I," said the Princess.

So he had found her once.

The second time the Princess turned herself into a loaf of bread, and laid herself on the table among four other loaves; and so like was she to the others, no one could say which was which.

But the lad went again down to the stable to Dapplegrim, and said how the Princess had hidden herself again, and he couldn't tell at all what had become of her.

"Oh, just take and sharpen a good bread knife," said Dapplegrim, "and do as if you were going to cut in two the third loaf on the left hand of those four loaves which are lying on the dresser in the King's kitchen, and you'll find her soon enough."

Yes! the lad was down in the kitchen in no time, and began to sharpen the biggest bread knife he could lay hands on. Then he caught hold of the third loaf on the left hand, and put the knife to it, as though he was going to cut it in two.

"I'll just have a slice off this loaf," he said.

"Nay, dear friend," said the Princess, "don't cut. It's I."

So he had found her twice.

Then he was to go and hide; but he and Dapplegrim had settled it all so well beforehand, it wasn't easy to find him.

First he turned himself into a tick, and hid himself in Dapplegrim's left nostril; and the Princess went about hunting him everywhere, high and low. At last she wanted to go into Dapplegrim's stall, but he began to bite and kick so that she daren't go near him, and so she couldn't find the lad.

"Well," she said, "since I can't find you, you must show where you are yourself"; and in a trice the lad stood there on the stable floor.

The second time Dapplegrim told him again what to do; and then he turned himself into a clod of earth, and stuck himself between Dapple's hoof and shoe on the near fore-foot. So the Princess hunted up and down, out and in, everywhere. At last she came into the stable, and wanted to go into Dapplegrim's loose-box. This time he let her come up to him, and she pried high and low, but under his hoofs she couldn't come, for he stood firm as a rock on his feet, and so she couldn't find the lad.

"Well; you must show yourself, for I'm sure I can't find you," said the Princess, and as she spoke the lad stood by her side on the stable floor.

"Now you are mine indeed," said the lad; "for now you can see I'm fated to have you." This he said both to the father and daughter.

"Yes; it is so fated," said the King; "so it must be."

Then they got ready the wedding in downright earnest, and lost no time about it. And the lad got on Dapplegrim, and the Princess on Dapplegrim's match, and then you may fancy they were not long on their way to the church.

FARMER WEATHERSKY

* * *

ONCE on a time there was a man and his wife, who had an only son, and his name was John. The old dame thought it high time for her son to go out into the world to learn a trade, and bade her husband be off with him.

"But whatever you do," she said, "mind you bind him to someone who can teach him to be master above all masters"; and with that she put some food and a roll of tobacco into a bag, and packed them off.

Well! they went to many masters; but one and all said they could make the lad as good as themselves, but better, they couldn't make him. So when the man came home again to his wife with that answer, she said,

"I don't care what you make of him; but this I say and stick to, you must bind him to someone where he can learn to be master above all masters"; and with that she packed up more food and another roll of tobacco, and father and son had to be off again.

Now when they had walked a while they got upon an ice-bound lake, and there they met a man who came whisking along in a sledge, driving a black horse.

"Whither away?" said the man.

"Well!" said the father, "I'm going to bind my son to someone who is able to teach him a trade; but my old dame comes of such fine folk that she will have him taught to be master above all masters."

"Well met, then," said the driver. "I'm just the man for your money, for I'm looking out for such an apprentice. Up with you, behind, he added to the lad, and whisk, off they went, both of them, sledge and horse, right up into the air.

"Nay, nay!" cried the lad's father; "you haven't told me your name, nor where you live."

"Oh!" said the master, "I'm at home alike, north and south, and east and west, and my name's Farmer Weathersky. In a year and a day you may come here again, and then I'll tell you what I think of him." So away they went through the air, and were soon out of sight.

So when the man got home, his old dame asked what had become of their son.

Well, said the man, "Heaven knows; I'm sure I don't. They went up aloft; and he told her what had happened. But when the old dame heard that her husband couldn't tell at all when her son's apprenticeship would be over, nor whither he had gone, she packed him off again, and gave him another bag of food and another roll of tobacco.

When he had walked a bit, he came to a great wood, which stretched on and on all day, as he walked through it. When it got dark he saw a great light, and he went towards it. After a long, long time he came to a little hut under a rock, and outside it stood an old hag, drawing water out of a well with her nose, so long was it.

"Good evening, mother!" said the man.

"The same to you," said the old hag. "It's hundreds of years since anyone called me mother."

"Can I have lodging here tonight?" asked the man.

"No! that you can't," said she.

But the man pulled out his roll of tobacco, lighted his pipe, and gave the old dame a whiff, and a pinch of snuff. She was so happy she began to dance for joy, and in the end, gave the man leave to stop for the night.

The next morning he began to ask after Farmer Weathersky. No! she had never heard tell of him, but as she ruled over all the four-footed beasts, perhaps some of them might know him. So she played them all home with a pipe she had, and asked them, but there wasn't one of them who knew anything about Farmer Weathersky.

"Well!" said the old hag, "there are three of us sisters; maybe one of the other two will know where he lives. I'll lend you my horse and sledge, and then you'll be at one of their houses by night, though it's at least three hundred miles off, the nearest way."

So the man started off, and at night reached the house, and when he came there, there stood another old hag before the door, drawing water out of the well with her nose.

"Good evening, mother!" said the man.

"The same to you," said she; "it's hundreds of years since anyone called me mother."

"Can I lodge here tonight?" asked the man.

"No!" said the old hag.

But he took out his roll of tobacco, lighted his pipe, and gave the old dame a whiff, and a good pinch of snuff besides, on the back of her hand. She was so happy that she began to jump and dance for joy, and so the man got leave to stay the night. When that night was over, he began to ask after Farmer Weathersky. No! she had never heard tell of him; but she ruled all the fish in the sea; perhaps some of them might know something about him. So she played them all home with a pipe she had, and asked them, but there wasn't one of them who knew anything about Farmer Weathersky.

"Well, well!" said the old hag, "there's one sister of us left; maybe she knows something about him. She lives six hundred miles off, but I'll lend you my horse and sledge, and then you'll get there by nightfall."

So the man started off, and reached the house by nightfall, and there he found another old hag who stood before the grate, and stirred the fire with her nose, so long and tough it was.

"Good evening, mother!" said the man.

"The same to you," said the old hag; "it's hundreds of years since anyone called me mother."

"Can I lodge here tonight?" asked the man.

"No," said the old hag.

Then the man pulled out his roll of tobacco again, and lighted his pipe, and gave the old hag such a pinch of snuff it covered the whole back of her hand. She was so happy she began to dance for joy, and so the man got leave to stay.

But when the night was over, he began to ask after Farmer Weathersky. She had never heard tell of him she said. But she ruled over all the birds of the air, and so she played them all home with a pipe she had, and when she had mustered them all, the eagle was missing. But a little while after he came flying home, and when she asked him, he said he had just come straight from Farmer Weathersky. So the old hag said he must guide the man thither. But the eagle said he must have something to eat first, and besides he must rest till the next day, he was so tired with flying that long way, he could scarce rise from the earth.

So when he had eaten his fill and taken a good rest, the old hag pulled a feather out of the eagle's tail, and put the man there in its stead. And the eagle flew off with the man, and they flew, and flew, but they didn't reach Farmer Weathersky's house before midnight.

When they got there, the eagle said,

"There are heaps of dead bodies lying about outside, but you mustn't mind them. Inside the house every man Jack of them are so sound asleep, it will be hard work to wake them. But you must go straight to the table drawer and take out of it three crumbs of bread, and when you hear someone snoring loud, pull three feathers out of his head, though he won't wake for all that."

So the man did as he was told, and after he had taken the crumbs of bread, he pulled out the first feather.

"OOF!" growled Farmer Weathersky, for it was he who snored.

So the man pulled out another feather.

"OOF!" he growled again.

But when he pulled out the third feather, Farmer Weathersky roared so loud, the man thought the roof and wall would have flown asunder, but for all that the snorer slept on.

After that the eagle told him what to do. He went to the yard, and there at the stable door he stumbled against a big gray stone, and that, he lifted up. Underneath it lay three chips of wood, and those he picked up too. Then he knocked at the stable door, and it opened of itself. He then threw down the three crumbs of bread, and a hare came and ate them up. That hare he caught and kept. After that the eagle bade him pull three feathers out of his tail, and put the hare, the stone, the chips, and himself there instead, and then he would fly away home with them all.

When the eagle had flown a long way, he alighted on a rock to rest.

"Do you see anything?" it asked.

"Yes," said the man, "I see a flock of crows coming flying after us."

"We'd better be off again, then," said the eagle, who flew away.

After a while it asked again,

"Do you see anything now?"

"Yes," said the man; "now the crows are close behind us."

"Drop now the three feathers you pulled out of Farmer Weathersky's head," said the eagle.

Well, the man dropped the feathers, and as soon as ever he dropped them, they became a flock of ravens which drove the crows home again. Then the eagle flew on again with the man, and at last it alighted on another stone to rest.

"Do you see anything?" it said.

"I'm not sure," said the man. "I fancy I see something coming far, far away."

"We'd better get on then," said the eagle; and after a while it asked again,

"Do you see anything?"

"Yes," said the man, "now Farmer Weathersky is close at our heels."

"Now, you must let fall the chips of wood which you took from under the gray stone at the stable door," said the eagle.

Yes! the man let them fall, and they grew up at once into tall thick woods, so that Farmer Weathersky had to go back home to fetch an axe to hew his way through. While he did this, the eagle flew ever so far, but when it got tired, it lighted on a fir to rest.

"Do you see anything?" it asked.

"Well, I'm not sure," said the man; "but I fancy I can catch a glimpse of something far away."

"We'd best be off then," said the eagle; and off it flew as fast as it could. After a while it said,

"Do you see anything now?"

"Yes! now he's close behind us," said the man.

"Now, drop the big stone you lifted up at the stable door," said the eagle.

The man did so, and as it fell, it became a great high mountain, through which Farmer Weathersky had to break his way. When he had got half through the mountain, he tripped and broke one of his legs, and so he had to limp home again and patch it up.

But while he was doing this, the eagle flew away to the man's house with him and the hare, and as soon as they got home, the man went into the churchyard and sprinkled Christian mould over the hare, and lo! it turned into John, his son.

Well, you may fancy that the old dame was glad to get her son again, but still she wasn't easy in her mind about his trade, and she wouldn't rest till he gave her proof that he was "master above all masters."

So when the fair came round, the lad changed himself into a bay horse, and told his father to lead him to the fair.

"Now, when anyone comes to buy me," he said, "you may ask a hundred dollars for me; but mind you don't forget to take the head-stall off me. If you do, Farmer Weathersky will keep me forever, for he it is who will come to deal with you.

So it turned out. Up came a horse dealer, who had a great wish to deal for the horse, and so gave a hundred dollars down for him. But when the bargain was struck, and John's father pocketed the money, the horse-dealer wanted to have the headstall. "Nay, nay!" said the man, "there's nothing about that in the bargain; and besides, you can't have the headstall, for I've other horses at home to bring to town tomorrow."

So each went his way; but they hadn't gone far before John took his own shape and ran away, and when his father got home, there sat John in the ingle.

Next day he turned himself into a brown horse, and told his father to drive him to the fair.

"And when anyone comes to buy me, you may ask two hundred dollars for me. He'll give that and treat you besides; but whatever you do, and however much you drink, don't forget to take the head-stall off me, else you'll never set eyes on me again."

So all happened as he said: the man got two hundred dollars for the horse and a glass of drink besides, and when the buyer and seller parted, it was as much as he could do to remember to take the headstall off. But the buyer and the horse hadn't gone far on the road before John took his own shape, and when the man got home, there sat John in the ingle.

The third day, it was the same story over again: the lad turned himself into a black horse, and told his father someone would come and bid three hundred dollars for him, and fill his skin with meat and drink besides; but however much he ate or drank, he was to mind and not forget to take the headstall off, else he'd have to stay with Farmer Weathersky all his life long.

"No, no, I'll not forget, never fear," said the man.

So when he came to the fair, he got three hundred dollars for the horse, and as it wasn't to be a dry bargain, Farmer Weathersky made him drink so much that he quite forgot to take the headstall off and away went Farmer Weathersky with the horse. Now when he had gone a little way, Farmer Weathersky thought he would just stop and have another glass of brandy. So he put a barrel of red hot nails under his horse's nose, and a sieve of oats under his tail, hung the halter upon a hook, and went into the inn. The horse stood there, and stamped and pawed, and snorted and reared. Just then out came a girl, who thought it a shame to treat a horse so.

"Oh, poor beastie," she said, "what a cruel master you must have to treat you so," and as she said this she pulled the halter off the hook, so that the horse might turn round and taste the oats.

"I'm after you," roared Farmer Weathersky, who came rushing out of the door.

But the horse had already shaken off the headstall, and jumped
into a duck pond, where he turned himself into a tiny fish. In went
Farmer Weathersky after him, and turned himself into a great pike.
Then John turned himself into a dove, and Farmer Weathersky
made himself into a hawk, and chased and struck at the dove. But
just then a Princess stood at the window of the palace and saw this
struggle.

"Ah! poor dove," she cried, "if you only knew what I know,
you'd fly to me through this window."

So the dove came flying in through the window, and turned
itself into John again, who told her his tale.

"Turn yourself into a gold ring, and put yourself on my finger,"
said the Princess.

"Nay, nay!" said John, "that'll never do, for then Farmer Weathersky will make the King sick, and then there'll be no one who can
make him well again till Farmer Weathersky comes and cures him,
and then, for his fee, he'll ask for that gold ring."

"Then I'll say I had it from my mother, and can't part with it,"
said the Princess.

Well, John turned himself into a gold ring, and put himself on
the Princess' finger, and so Farmer Weathersky couldn't get at him.
But then followed what the lad had foretold; the King fell sick, and
there wasn't a doctor in the kingdom who could cure him till Farmer
Weathersky came, and he asked for the ring off the Princess' finger
for his fee. So the King sent a messenger to the Princess for the ring;
but the Princess said she wouldn't part with it, for her mother had
left it her. When the King heard that, he flew into a rage, and said
he would have the ring, whoever left it to her.

"Well," said the Princess, "it's no good being cross about it. I
can't get it off, and if you must have the ring, you must take my
finger too."

"If you'll let me try, I'll soon get the ring off," said Farmer Weathersky.

"No, thanks, I'll try, myself," said the Princess, and flew off to the grate and put ashes on her finger. Then the ring slipped off and was lost among the ashes. So Farmer Weathersky turned himself into a cock, who scratched and pecked after the ring in the grate, till he was up to his ears in ashes. But while he was doing this, John turned himself into a fox, and bit off the cock's head. And so, if the Evil One was in Farmer Weathersky, it is all over with him now.

THE GIANT WHO HAD
NO HEART IN HIS BODY

* * *

ONCE on a time there was a king who had seven sons, and he loved
them so much that he could never bear to be without them all at
once, but one must always be with him. Now, when they were
grown up, six were to set off to woo, but as for the youngest, his
father kept him at home, and the others were to bring back a princess for him to the palace. So the king gave the six the finest clothes
you ever set eyes on, so fine that the light gleamed from them a long
way off, and each had his horse, which cost many, many hundred
dollars, and so they set off. Now, when they had been to many pal-
aces, and seen many princesses, at last they came to a king who had
six daughters; such lovely king's daughters they had never seen, and
so they fell to wooing them, each one, and when they had got them
for sweethearts, they set off home again. But they quite forgot that
they were to bring back with them a sweet-heart for the Ashlad,
their brother, who stayed at home, for they were over head and ears
in love with their own sweet-hearts.

But when they had gone a good bit on their way, they passed
close by a steep hillside, like a wall, where the Giant's house was,
and there the Giant came out, and set his eyes upon them, and
turned them all into stone, princes and princesses and all. But the

King waited and waited for his six sons, but the more he waited, the longer they stayed away; so he fell into great trouble, and said he would never know what it was to be glad again.

"And if I did not have you," he said to the Ashlad, "I would live no longer, so full of sorrow am I for the loss of your brothers."

"Well, but I've been thinking of asking your leave to set out to find them again; that's what I'm thinking of doing," said the Ashlad.

"Nay, nay!" said his father; "that leave you shall never get, for then you too, would stay away."

But the Ashlad had set his heart upon it; go he would; and he begged and prayed so long that the King was forced to let him go. Now, you must know the King had no other horse to give him but an old broken down jade, for his six other sons and their train had carried off all his horses. But the Ashlad did not care a pin for that; he sprang up on his sorry old steed.

"Farewell, father," said he; "I'll come back, never fear, and like enough I shall bring my six brothers back with me"; and with that he rode off.

When he had ridden a while, he came to a raven. It lay in the road and flapped its wings, and was not able to get out of the way, it was so starved.

"Oh, dear friend," said the raven, "give me a little food, and in return, I'll help you in your utmost need."

"I haven't much food," said the Prince, "and I don't see how you'll ever be able to help me much; but still I can spare you a little. I see you need it."

So he gave the raven some of the food he had brought.

Now, when he had gone a bit farther, he came to a brook, and in the brook lay a great salmon, which had got upon a dry place and dashed itself about, and could not get into the water again.

"Oh, dear friend," said the salmon to the Prince; "shove me out into the water again, and I'll help you again at your utmost need."

"Well!" said the Prince, "the help you'll give me will not be great, I daresay, but it's a pity you should lie there and choke"; and with that he shot the fish out into the stream again.

After that he went a long, long way, and there met him a wolf, which was so famished that it lay and crawled along the road on its belly.

"Dear friend, do let me have your horse," said the wolf; "I'm so hungry, the wind whistles through my ribs; I've had nothing to eat these two years."

"No," said the Ashlad, "this will never do; first I came to a raven, and I was forced to give him my food; next I came to a salmon, and him I had to help into the water again; and now you will have my horse. It can't be done, that it can't, for then I should have nothing to ride on."

"Nay, dear friend, but you can help me," said Graylegs, the wolf. "You can ride upon my back, and I'll help you again in your utmost need."

"Well! the help I shall get from you will not be great, I'll be bound," said the Prince; "but you may take my horse, since you are in such need."

So when the wolf had eaten the horse, the Prince took the bit and put it into the wolf's jaw, and laid the saddle on his back. And now the wolf was so strong, after what he had put inside him that he set off with the Prince faster than he had ever ridden before.

"When we have gone a bit farther," said Graylegs, "I'll show you the Giant's house."

After a while they came to it.

"See, here is the Giant's house," said the wolf. "And see, there are your six brothers, whom the Giant turned into stone; and here

are their six brides; and away yonder is the door, and in at that door you must go."

"Nay, but I daren't go in," said the Prince. "He'll take my life."

"No, no!" said the wolf. "When you get in you'll find a princess, and she'll tell you what to do to make an end of the Giant. Only mind and do as she bids you."

Well! the Ashlad went in, though he was very much afraid. When he came in the Giant was away, but in one of the rooms sat the Princess, just as the wolf had said, and so lovely a princess the Ashlad had never set eyes on.

"Oh! Heaven help you! Whence have you come?" said the Princess, as she saw him. "It will surely be your death. No one can make an end of the Giant who lives here, for he has no heart in his body."

"Well! well!" said the Ashlad, "now that I am here, I may as well try what I can do with him. I will see if I can't free my brothers, who are standing turned to stone out of doors; and you, too, I will try to save; that I will."

"Well, if you must, you must," said the Princess; "and so let us see if we can't hit on a plan. Just creep under the bed yonder, and mind and listen to what he and I talk about. But, pray, do lie as still as a mouse."

So he crept under the bed, and he had scarce got well underneath it, before the Giant came in.

"Ha!" roared the Giant. "What a smell of Christian blood there is in the house!"

"Yes, I know there is," said the Princess, "for there came a magpie flying with a man's bone, and let it fall down chimney. I made all the haste I could to get it out, but in spite of all one can do, the smell doesn't go off soon."

So the Giant said no more about it, and when night came, they went to bed. After they had lain a while the Princess said,

"There is one thing I'd be so glad to ask you about, if I only dared."

"What thing is that?" asked the Giant.

"Only where it is you keep your heart, since you don't carry it about with you," said the Princess.

"Ah! that's a thing you've no business to ask about; but if you must know, it lies under the doorsill," said the Giant.

"Ho! ho!" said the Ashlad to himself under the bed, "then we'll soon see if we can't find it."

Next morning the Giant got up cruelly early, and strode off to the wood. But he was hardly out of the house before the Ashlad and the Princess set to work to look under the doorsill for his heart; but the more they dug, and the more they hunted, the more they couldn't find it.

"He has balked us this time," said the Princess, "but we'll try him once more."

So she picked all the prettiest flowers she could find, and strewed them over the doorsill, which they had laid in its right place again. And when the time came for the Giant to come home again, the Ashlad crept under the bed. Just as he was well under it, back came the Giant.

Snuff, snuff went the Giant's nose. "Faugh, what a smell of Christian blood there is in here," said he.

"I know there is," said the Princess, "for there came a magpie flying with a man's bone in his bill, and let it fall down the chimney. I made as much haste as I could to get it out, but I daresay it's that you smell."

So the Giant held his peace, and said no more about it. A little while after, he asked who it was that had strewn flowers about the door sill.

"Oh, I of course," said the Princess.

"And, pray, what's the meaning of all this?" said the Giant.

"Ah!" said the Princess, "I'm so fond of you that I couldn't help strewing them, when I knew that your heart lay under there."

"You don't say so!" said the Giant. "But after all, it doesn't lie there at all."

So when they went to bed again in the evening, the Princess asked the Giant again where his heart was, for she said she would so like to know.

"Well," said the Giant, "if you must know, it lies away yonder in the cupboard against the wall."

"So, so!" thought the Ashlad and the Princess; "then we'll soon try to find it."

Next morning the Giant was away early, and strode off to the wood, and so soon as he was gone the Ashlad and the Princess were in the cupboard hunting for his heart, but the more they sought for it, the less they found it.

"Well," said the Princess, "we'll just try him once more."

So she decked out the cupboard with flowers and garlands, and when the time came for the Giant to come home, the Ashlad crept under the bed again.

Then back came the Giant.

Snuff, snuff! "Faugh, what a smell of Christian blood there is in here!"

"I know there is," said the Princess, "for a little while since there came a magpie flying with a man's bone in his bill, and let it fall down the chimney. I made all the haste I could to get it out of the house again; but after all my pains, I daresay it's that you smell."

When the Giant heard that, he said no more about it; but a little while after, he saw how the cupboard was all decked about with flowers and garlands. So he asked who it was that had done that? Who could it be but the Princess?

"And, pray, what's the meaning of all this tomfoolery?" asked the Giant.

"Oh, I'm so fond of you, I couldn't help doing it when I knew that your heart lay there," said the Princess.

"How can you be so silly as to believe any such thing?" said the Giant.

"Oh, yes; how can I help believing it, when you say it?" said the Princess.

"You're a goose," said the Giant; "where my heart is, you will never come."

"Well," said the Princess; "but for all that, I'd like to know where it really is."

Then the Giant could hold out no longer, but was forced to say,

"Far, far away in a lake lies an island; on that island stands a church; in that church, is a well; in that well, swims a duck; in that duck, there is an egg, and in that egg there lies my heart."

In the morning early, while it was still grey dawn, the Giant strode off to the wood.

"Yes! now I must set off too," said the Ashlad. "If I only knew how to find the way!" He then took leave of the Princess, and when he got out of the Giant's door, there stood the wolf waiting for him. So the Ashlad told him all that had happened inside the house, and how he wished to ride to the well in the church, if he only knew the way. So the wolf bade him jump on his back; he'd soon find the way. Away they went, till the wind whistled after them, over hedge and field, over hill and dale. After they had travelled many, many days, they came at last to the lake. The Prince did not know how to get over it, but the wolf bade him not be afraid, but to stick on, and so he jumped into the lake with the Prince on his back, and swam over to the island. So they came to the church; but the church keys hung high, high up on the top of the tower, and at first the Prince did not know how to get them down.

"You must call on the raven," said the wolf.

So the Prince called on the raven, and in a trice the raven came, and flew up and fetched the keys, and so the Prince got into the church. But when he came to the well, there lay the duck, and swam about backwards and forwards, just as the Giant had said. So the Prince stood and coaxed it and coaxed it, till it came to him, when he grasped it in his hand; but just as he lifted it up from the water, the duck dropped the egg into the well, and then the Ashlad was beside himself to know how to get it out again.

"Well, now you must call on the salmon, to be sure," said the wolf. So the king's son called on the salmon, and the salmon came and fetched up the egg from the bottom of the well.

Then the wolf told him to squeeze the egg, and as soon as ever he squeezed it, the Giant screamed out.

"Squeeze it again," said the wolf; and when the Prince did so, the Giant screamed still more piteously, and begged and prayed so prettily to be spared, saying he would do all that the Prince wished if he would only not squeeze his heart in two.

"Tell him, if he will restore to life again your six brothers and their brides, whom he has turned to stone, you will spare his life," said the wolf. Yes, the Giant was ready to do that, and he turned the six brothers into king's sons again, and their brides into king's daughters.

"Now, squeeze the egg in two," said the wolf. So the Ashlad squeezed the egg to pieces, and the Giant burst.

Now, when he had made an end of the Giant, the Ashlad rode back again on the wolf to the Giant's house, and there stood all his six brothers alive and merry, with their brides. Then the Ashlad went into the hillside after his bride, and so they all set off home again to their father's house. And you may fancy how glad the old King was when he saw all his seven sons come back, each with his bride. "But the loveliest bride of all is the bride of the Ashlad, after all," said the King; "and he shall sit uppermost at the table, with her by his side."

So he sent out, and called a great wedding feast, and the mirth was both loud and long. And if they have not done feasting, why, they are still at it.

THE BIG BIRD DAN

* * *

ONCE on a time there was a king who had twelve daughters, and he was so fond of them they must always be at his side; but every day at noon, while the King slept, the Princesses went out to take a walk. So once, while the King was taking his noontide nap, and the Princesses had gone to take their walk, all at once they were missing, and worse, they never came home again. Then there was great grief and sorrow all over the land, but the most sorry of all was the King. He sent messengers out throughout his own and other realms, and gave out their names in all the churches, and had the bells tolled for them in all the steeples; but gone the Princesses were, and gone they stayed, and none could tell what was become of them. So it was as clear as day that they must have been carried off by some witchcraft.

Well, it wasn't long before these tidings spread far and wide, over land and town, aye, over many lands; and so the news came to a king ever so many lands away who had twelve sons. So when these Princes heard of the King's twelve daughters, they asked leave of their father to go out and seek them. They had hard work to get his leave, for he was afraid lest he should never see them again, but they all fell down on their knees before the King, and begged so long, at last he was forced to let them go after all.

He fitted out a ship for them, and gave them the Red Knight, who was a good skipper, for a captain. So they sailed about a long, long time, landed on every shore they came to, and hunted and asked after the Princesses, but they could neither hear nor see anything of them. And now, a few days only were wanting to make up seven years since they set sail, when one day a strong storm rose, and such foul weather, they thought they should never come to land again, and all had to work so hard, they couldn't get a wink of sleep so long as the storm lasted. But when the third day was nearly over, the wind fell, and all at once it got as still as still could be. Now, they were all so weary with work and the rough weather, they fell fast asleep in the twinkling of an eye; all but the youngest Prince, he could get no rest, and couldn't go off to sleep at all.

So as he was pacing up and down the deck, the ship came to a little island, and on the island ran a little dog. He bayed and barked at the ship as if he wanted to come on board. So the Prince went to that side of the deck, and tried to coax the dog, and whistled and whistled to him, but the more he whistled, and coaxed, the more the dog barked and snarled. Well, he thought it a shame the dog should run about there and starve, for he made up his mind that it must have come thither from a ship that had been cast away in the storm; but still he thought he should never be able to help it after all, for he couldn't put out the boat by himself, and as for the others, they all slept so sound, he wouldn't wake them for the sake of a dog. But then the weather was so calm and still; and at last he said to himself; "Come what may, you must go ashore and save that dog," and so he began to try to launch the boat, and he found it far easier work than he thought. So he rowed ashore, and went up to the dog; but every time he tried to catch it, it jumped on one side, and so it went on till he found himself inside a great grand castle, before he knew where he was.

Then the dog, all at once was changed into a lovely Princess; and there, on the bench, sat a man so big and ugly, the Prince almost lost his wits for fear.

"You've no need to be afraid," said the man—but the Prince, to tell you the truth, got far more afraid when he heard his gruff voice—"for I know well enough what you want. There are twelve Princes of you, and you are looking for the twelve Princesses that are lost. I know, too, very well, whereabouts they are; they're with my lord and master, and there they sit, each of them on her chair, and comb his hair; for he has twelve heads. And now you have sailed seven years, but you'll have to sail seven years more before you find them. As for you, you might stay here and welcome, and have my daughter; but you must first slay him, for he's a hard master to all of us, and we're all weary of him, and when he's dead I shall be King in his stead; but first try if you can brandish this sword."

Then the King's son took hold of a rusty old sword which hung on the wall, but he could scarce stir it.

"Now you must take a pull at this flask," said the troll; and when he had done that he could stir it, and when he had taken another he could lift it, and when he had taken a third he could brandish the sword as easily as if it had been his own.

"Now, when you get on board," said the troll Prince, "you must hide the sword well in your berth, that the Red Knight mayn't set eyes on it; he's not man enough to wield it, but he'll get spiteful against you, and try to take your life. And when seven years are almost out, all but three days," he went on to say, "everything will happen just as now; foul weather will some on you, with a great storm, and when it is over you'll all be sleepy. Then you must take the sword and row ashore, and you'll come to a castle where all sorts of guards will stand—wolves, and bears, and lions; but you needn't be afraid of hem, for they'll all come and crouch at your feet. But when you come inside the castle, you'll soon see the troll; he sits in splendid chamber in grand attire and array; twelve heads he has of his own, and the Princesses sit round them, each on her hair, and comb his heads, and that's a work you may guess they don't much like. Then you must make haste, and hew off the head after the other as quick as you can; for if he wakes and sets his eyes on you, he'll swallow you alive."

So the King's son went on board with the sword, and he bore in mind what he had come to know. The others still lay fast asleep and snored, and he hid the sword in his berth, so that neither the Red Knight nor any of the rest got sight of it. And now it began to blow again, so he woke up the others and said he thought they oughtn't to sleep any longer now when there was such a good wind. And there was none of them that remarked he had been away. Well, after the seven years were all gone but three days, all happened as the troll had said. A great storm and foul weather came on that lasted three days, and when it had blown itself out, all the rest grew sleepy and went to rest; but the King's youngest son rowed ashore, and the guards fell at his feet, and so he came to the castle. So when he got inside the chamber, there sat the King fast asleep as the troll Prince had said, and the twelve Princesses sat each on her chair and combed one of his heads. The King's son beckoned to the Princesses to get out of the way; they pointed to the troll, and beckoned to him again to go his way as quick as ever he could, but he kept on making signs to them to get out of the way, and then they understood that he wanted to set them free, and stole away softly one after the other, and as fast as they went, he hewed off the troll King's heads, till at last the blood gushed out like a great brook. When the troll was slain he rowed on board and hid his sword. He thought now he had done enough, and as he couldn't get rid of the body by himself, he thought it only fair they should help him a little. So he woke them all up, and said it was a shame they would be snoring there, when he had found the Princesses, and set them free from the troll. The others only laughed at him, and said he had been just as sound asleep as they, and only dreamt that he was man enough to do what he said; for if anyone was to set the Princesses free, it was far more likely it would be one of them. But the King's youngest son told them all about it, and when they followed him to the land saw first of all the brook of blood, and then the castle, and the troll, and the twelve heads, and the Princesses, they saw plain enough that he had spoken the truth, and now the whole helped him to throw the body and the heads into the sea. So all were glad and happy, but none more so than the Princesses, who got rid of having to sit there and comb the troll's hair all day. Of all the silver and gold and precious things that were there, they took as much as the ship could hold, and so they went on board altogether, Princes and Princesses alike.

But when they had gone a bit out on the sea, the Princesses said they had forgotten in their joy their gold crowns; they lay behind in a press, and they would be so glad to have them. So when none of the others were willing to fetch them, the King's youngest son said,

"I have already dared so much, I can very well go back for the gold crowns too, if you will only strike sail and wait till I come again."

Yes, that they would do. But when he had gone back so far that they couldn't see him any longer, the Red Knight, who would have been glad enough to have been their chief, and to have the youngest Princess, said it was no use their lying there still waiting for him, for they might know very well he would never come back; they all knew, too, how the King had given him all power and authority to sail or not as he chose; and now they must all say 'twas he that had saved the Princesses, and if anyone said anything else, he should lose his life.

The Princes didn't dare to do anything else than what the Red Knight willed, and so they sailed away.

Meanwhile, the King's youngest son rowed to land, went up to the castle, found the press with the gold crowns in it, and at last lugged it down to the boat, and shoved off; but when he came where he ought to have seen the ship, lo! it was gone. Well, as he couldn't catch a glimpse of it anywhere, he could very soon tell how matters stood. To row after them was no good, and so he was forced to turn about and row back to land. He was rather afraid to stay alone in the castle all night, but there was no other house to go to so he plucked up a heart, locked up all the doors and gates fast, and lay down in a room where there was a bed ready made. But fearful and woeful he was, and still more afraid he got when he had lain a while and something began to creak and groan and quake in wall and roof, as if the whole castle were being torn asunder. Then all at once down something plunged close by the side of his bed, as if it were a whole cartload of hay. Then all was still again; but after a while he heard a voice, which bade him not to be afraid, and said,

"Here am I the Big Bird Dan;
Come to help you all I can.

but the first thing you must do when you wake in the morning, will be to go to the barn and fetch four barrels of rye for me. I must fill my crop with them for breakfast, else I can't do anything."

When he woke up, sure enough there he saw an awfully big bird, which had a feather at the nape of his neck, as thick and long as a half-grown spruce-fir. So the King's son went down to the barn to fetch four barrels of rye for the Big Bird Dan, and when he had crammed them into his crop he told the King's son to hang the press with the gold crowns on one side of his neck, and as much gold and silver as would weigh it down on the other side, and after that to get on his back and hold fast by the feather in the nape of his neck. So away they went till the wind whistled after them, and so it wasn't long before they outstripped the ship. The King's son wanted to go on board for his sword, for he was afraid lest anyone should get sight of it, for the troll had told him that mustn't be; but the Big Bird Dan said that mustn't be either.

"The Red Knight will never see it, never fear; but if you go on board, he'll try to take your life, for he has set his heart on having the youngest Princess. But make your mind quite easy about her, for she lays a naked sword by her side in bed every night."

So after a long, long time, they came to the island where the troll Prince was; and there the King's son was welcomed so heartily there was no end to it. The troll Prince didn't know how to be good enough to him for having slain his Lord and Master, and so made him King of the trolls, and if the King's son had been willing he might easily have got the troll King's daughter, and half the kingdom. But he had so set his heart on the youngest of the twelve Princesses, he could take no rest, but was all for going after their ship time after time. So the troll King begged him to be quiet a little longer, and said they had still nearly seven years to sail before they got home. As for the Princess the troll said the same thing as the Big Bird Dan.

"You needn't fret yourself about her, for she lays a naked sword by her side every night in bed. And now if you don't believe what I say," said the troll, "you can go on board when; they sail by here, and see for yourself, and fetch the sword too, for I may just as well have it again."

So when they sailed by, another great storm arose, and when the King's son went on board they all slept, and each Princess lay beside her Prince; but the youngest lay alone with a naked sword

beside her in the bed, and on the floor by the bedside lay the Red
Knight. Then the king's son took the sword and rowed ashore again,
and none of them had seen that he had been on board. But still the
King's son couldn't rest, and he often and often wanted to be off, and
so at last when it got near the end of the seven years, and only three
weeks were left, the troll King said,

"Now, you may get ready to go since you won't stay with us;
and you shall have the loan of my iron boat, which sails of itself, if
you only say,

'*Boat, boat, go on!*'

"In that boat there is an iron club, and that club you must lift
a little when you see the ship straight ahead of you and then they'll
get such a rattling fair breeze, they'll forget to look at you; but when
you get alongside them, you must lift the club a little again, and then
they'll get such a foul wind and storm, they'll have something else
to do than to stare at you; and when you have run past them, you
must lift the club a third time, but you must always be sure to lay it
down carefully again, else there'll be such a storm both you and they
will be wrecked and lost. Now, when you have got to land, you've
no need to bother yourself at all about the boat; just turn it about,
and shove it off, and say,

'*Boat, boat, go back home!*'"

When he set out they gave him so much gold and silver, and
so many other costly things, and clothes and linen which the troll
Princess had sewn and woven for him all that long time, that he was
far richer than any of his brothers.

Well, he had no sooner seated himself in the boat, and said,

"Boat, boat, go on!"

than away went the boat, and when he saw the ship right ahead, he lifted up the club, and then they got such a fair breeze, they forgot to look at him. When he was alongside the ship, he lifted the club again, and then such a storm arose and such foul weather, that the white foam flew about the ship, and the billows rolled over the deck, and they had something else to do than to stare at him; and when he had run past them he lifted the club the third time, and then the storm and the wind rose so they had still less time to look after him, and to make him out. So he came to land long, long before the ship; and when he had got all his goods out of the boat, he shoved it off again, and turned it about and said,

"Boat, boat, go back home!"

And off went the boat.

Then he dressed himself up as a sailor—whether the troll King had told him that, or it was his own device, I'm sure I can't say—and went up to a wretched hut where an old wife lived, whom he got to believe that he was a poor sailor who had been on board a great ship that was wrecked, and that he was the only soul that had got ashore. After that he begged for houseroom for himself and the goods he had saved.

"Heaven mend me"; said the old wife, "how can I lend anyone houseroom? Look at me and mine. Why, I've no bed to sleep on myself, still less one for anyone else to lie on."

Well, well, it was all the same, said the sailor; if he only got a roof over his head, it didn't matter where he lay. So she couldn't turn him out of the house, when he was so thankful for what there was. That afternoon he fetched up his things, and the old wife, who was very eager to hear a bit of news to run about and tell, began at once to ask who he was, whence he came, whither he was bound, what it was he had with him, what his business was, and if he hadn't heard anything of the twelve Princesses who had been away the Lord knew how many years. All this she asked and much more, which it would be a waste of time to tell. But he said he was so poorly and had such a bad headache after the awful weather he had been out in, that he couldn't answer any of her questions; she must just leave him alone and let him rest a few days till he came to himself after the hard work he'd had in the gale, and then she'd know all she wanted.

The very next day the old wife began to stir him up and as again, but the sailor's head was still so bad he hadn't got his wits together, but somehow he let drop a word or two to show that he did know something about the Princesses. Off ran the old wife with what she had heard to all the gossips and chatterboxes round about, and soon the one came running after the other to ask about the Princesses, "if he had seen them, if they would soon be there," "if they were on the way," and much more of the same sort. He still went on groaning over his headache after the storm, so that he couldn't tell them all about it, but so much he told them, unless they had been lost in the great storm they'd make the land in about a fortnight or before per- haps; but he couldn't say for sure whether they were alive or no, for though he had seen them, it might very well be that they had been cast away in the storm since. So what did one of these old gossips do but run up to the Palace with this story, and say that there was a sailor down in such and such an old wife's hut, who had seen the Princesses, and that they were coming home in a fortnight or in a week's time. When the King heard that, he sent a messenger down to the sailor to come up to him and tell the news himself.

"I don't see how it's to be," said the sailor, "for I haven't any clothes fit to stand in before the King."

But the King said he must come; for the King must and would talk with him, whether he were richly or poorly clad, for there was no one else who could bring him any tidings of the Princesses. So he went up at last to the Palace and went in before the King, who asked him if it were true that he had seen anything of the Princesses.

"Aye, aye," said the sailor, "I've seen them sure enough, but I don't know whether they're still alive, for when I last caught sight of them, the weather was so foul we in our ship were cast away; but if they're still alive, they'll come safe home in a fortnight or perhaps before."

When the King heard that he was almost beside himself for joy; and when the time came that the sailor had said they would come, the King drove down to the strand to meet them in great state; and there was joy and gladness over the whole land, when the ship came sailing in with the Princes and Princesses and the Red Knight. But no one was gladder than the old King, who had got his daughters back again. The eleven eldest Princesses too, were glad and merry, but the youngest who was to have the Red Knight, who said that he had set them all free and slain the troll, she wept and was always sorrowful. The King took this ill, and asked why she wasn't cheerful and merry like the others; she hadn't anything to be sorry for now when she had got out of the troll's clutches, and was to have such a husband as the Red Knight. But she daren't say anything, for the Red Knight had said he would take the life of anyone who told the truth how things had gone.

But now one day, when they were hard at work sewing and stitching the bridal array, in came a man in a great sailor's cloak with a pedlar's pack on his back, and asked if the Princesses wouldn't buy something fine of him for the wedding; he had so many wares and costly things, both gold and silver. Yes, they might do so perhaps, so they looked at his wares and they looked at him, for they thought they had seen both him and many of his costly things before.

"He who has so many fine things," said the youngest Princess, "must surely have something still more precious, and which suits us better even than these."

"Maybe I have," said the pedlar.

But now all the others cried "Hush," and bade her bear in mind what the Red Knight had said he would do.

Well, some time after, the Princesses sat and looked out of the window, and then the King's son came again with the great sea-cloak thrown about him, and the press with gold crowns at his back; and when he got into the palace hall he unlocked the press before the Princesses, and when each of them knew her own gold crown again, the youngest said,

"I think it only right that he who set us free should get the meed that is his due; and he is not the Red Knight, but this man who has brought us our gold crowns. He it is that set us free."

Then the King's son cast off the sailor's cloak, and stood there far finer and grander than all the rest; and so the old King made them put the Red Knight to death. And now there was real downright joy in the palace; each took his own bride, and there really was a wedding! Why, it was heard of and talked about over twelve kings' realms.

THE BOY WITH THE ALE KEG

* * *

ONCE there was a boy who had served for a long time with a man of the North country. That man was past master at brewing beer, his ale was so incredibly good it was quite matchless. When the boy was about to leave and the man had to pay him his wages he said he wanted nothing but a keg of the Christmas ale. Well, he got it and went his way, and he carried it with him for a long time. But the longer he carried it, the heavier the ale keg felt, and he began to look about him, he might meet someone he would want to drink with, so that the keg would be somewhat lighter.

After a long while he met an old man with a long beard.

Good day, said the man.

"Good day to you," said the boy.

"Where are you going?" said the man.

"I am looking for somebody to drink with, so that my ale keg will be somewhat lighter," said the boy.

"Could you not drink with me just as well as with somebody else?" said the man. "I have come a long way, and I am both tired and thirsty."

"I could, said the boy, but where are you from, and what sort of a man are you then?"

"I am the Lord, I come from the kingdom of Heaven," said the man.

"You I will not drink with," said the boy, "because you make people so unequal here in this world, and you do not let them have equal justice—some you permit to become so rich, and some so lowly. No, I will not drink with you," he said, and jogged on with his ale keg.

When he had walked somewhat more, the keg again felt so heavy, it seemed to him he could not carry it any longer, unless he met somebody with whom he could drink and make the ale sink somewhat in the keg. Well, then he met an ugly, lean man, who came along in a terrible hurry.

"Good day," said the man.

"Good day to you," said the boy.

"Where are you going?" said the man.

"Oh, I am looking for somebody to drink with, to lighten this ale keg I carry, just a little," said the boy.

"Could you not drink with me as well as with somebody else?" said the man. "I have travelled far and wide, and a drink of ale would do good to my old body," he said.

"I could," said the boy, "but who are you, and where do you come from?" he asked.

"I? I am well known, I am the Devil, and I am coming from Hell," said the man.

"No," said the boy, "you do nothing but torture and plague people, and wherever mischief is afoot they always say, you are to blame. No, I will not drink with you," said the boy.

Then he walked on a long, long time with his ale keg, till it seemed to the boy the keg was so heavy, he could not possibly carry it any longer. He took to looking about him again, if he were not going to meet somebody with whom he could drink, so that the keg might become lighter. Well, after a long time a man came along, and he was so dry and bony, it was a miracle his limbs hung together.

"Good day," said the man.

"Good day to you," said the boy.

"Where are you going?" said the man.

"I am looking for somebody with whom I could drink, so this keg of mine might become a little lighter; it is terribly heavy to carry," said the boy.

"Could you not drink with me as well as with another body?" said the man.

"I could," said the boy, "but who are you then?"

"They call me Death," said the man.

"Yes, I will drink with you," said the boy. He laid down the ale keg and let the ale run into the bowl. "You are an honorable man, for you make everybody equal, rich and poor."

So he plied him, and Death thought this was a wonderful drink, and as the boy was glad to treat him, they plied each other till the ale sank in the keg and the keg had become quite light.

At last Death said: "Never did I taste a drink that was better or did me so much good as the ale you have poured me. I feel as if I had been born anew inside, and I do not know what I must do for you, to thank you for it." But after he had pondered for a while he said, the keg was never to become empty, however much was drunk from it; that the ale in it was to become a tonic to restore health to the sick, so that the boy would be able to cure them better than any doctor. And then he said that when the boy entered a sickroom Death would always be there, visible to the boy. And this was to be a sure sign for him to go by—when Death sat by the feet of the sick, the boy would be able to save him by a drink from the keg, but if he sat by the head of the bed, there was no help or remedy against death.

The boy soon became famous and was sent for from far away, and there was no counting of all the sick he restored to health, after they had been given up as hopeless. When he entered a room and saw where Death sat by the sick, he foretold life or death and he never was mistaken. He became a rich man and a powerful man, and at last he was called to a King's daughter in a country far away. She was so dangerously ill that no doctor believed anything could save her and so they promised him whatever he wanted if he was able to save her life. When he came in to the King's daughter Death sat by the head of her bed; but he sat and nodded and seemed to sleep, and as long as he sat like that, she felt easier. "This is a case of life or death," said the doctor. "But if I am right, there is no hope to save her." But they said he had to save her, if it were to cost the kingdom and country. Then he looked at Death, and whilst he sat nodding and sleeping, the doctor made a sign to the servants, they must turn the bed quickly, so that Death sat at the feet, and the moment they had done this he gave her the healing drink, and she was saved.

"Now you betrayed me," said Death, "and now we are quits."

"I had to do it, if I was to win a kingdom," said the boy.

"It is not going to help you much," said Death. "Your time is up, for now you belong to me."

"Well, if it has to be, it has to be," said the boy. "But you will give me leave to say the Lord's Prayer to the finish first?"

Yes, he was given leave to do that. But he took good care never to say the Lord's Prayer. Whatever he said, the Lord's Prayer never came in his mouth, and in the end he imagined he had cheated Death. But when Death thought this had lasted too long, he went to him one night and put up a big board with the Lord's Prayer written upon it, in front of his bed. When he awoke he started reading it, and he was not aware of what he was doing till he reached the amen; but then it was too late.

THE BLACKSMITH THEY WERE
AFRAID TO RECEIVE IN HELL

* * *

ONCE on a time, in the days when our Lord and St. Peter used to wander on earth, they came to a smith's house. He had made a bargain with the Devil that the fiend should have him after seven years, but during that time he was to be master of all masters in his trade, and to this bargain both he and the Devil had signed their names. So he had struck up in great letters over the door of his forge,

HERE DWELLS THE MASTER OVER ALL MASTERS.

Now, when our Lord passed by and saw that, he went in.

"Who are you?" he said to the Smith.

"Read what's written over the door," said the Smith; "but maybe you can't read writing. If so, you must wait till someone comes to help you."

Before our Lord had time to answer him, a man came with his horse, which he begged the Smith to shoe.

"Might I have leave to shoe it?" asked our Lord.

"You may try, if you like," said the Smith; "you can't do it so badly that I shall not be able to make it right again."

So our Lord went out and took one leg off the horse, and laid it in the furnace, and made the shoe red-hot; after that, he turned up the ends of the shoe, and filed down the heads of the nails, and clenched the points; and then he put back the leg safe and sound on the horse again. And when he was done with that leg, he took the other foreleg and did the same with it; and when he was done with that, he took the hind legs—first, the off, and then the near leg, and laid them in the furnace, making the shoes red-hot, turning up the ends, filing the heads of the nails, and clenching the points; and after all was done, putting the legs on the horse again. All the while, the Smith stood by and looked on.

"You're not so bad a smith after all," said he.

"Oh, you think so, do you?" said our Lord.

A little while after came the Smith's mother to the forge, and called him to come home and eat his dinner. She was an old, old woman with an ugly crook on her back, and wrinkles in her face, and it was as much as she could do to crawl along.

"Mark now, what you see," said our Lord.

Then he took the woman and laid her in the furnace, and smithied a lovely young maiden out of her.

"Well," said the Smith, "I say now, as I said before, you are not such a bad smith after all. There it stands over my door. 'Here dwells the Master over all Masters'; but for all that, I say right out, one learns as long as one lives"; and with that he walked off to his house and ate his dinner.

So after dinner, just after he had got back to his forge, a man came riding up to have his horse shod.

"It shall be done in the twinkling of an eye," said the Smith, "for I have just learnt a new way to shoe; and a very good way it is when the days are short."

So he began to cut and hack till he had got all the horse's legs off, for he said, "I don't know why one should go pottering backwards and forwards—first, with one leg, and then with another."

Then he laid the legs in the furnace, just as he had seen our Lord lay them, and threw on a great heap of coal, and made his mates work the bellows bravely; but it went as one might suppose it would go. The legs were burnt to ashes, and the Smith had to pay for the horse.

Well, he didn't care much about that, but just then an old beggar-woman came along the road, and he thought to himself, "better luck next time"; so he took the old dame and laid her in the furnace, and though she begged and prayed hard for her life, it was no good.

"You're so old, you don't know what is good for you," said the Smith; "now you shall be a lovely young maiden in half no time, and for all that, I'll not charge you a penny for the job."

But it went no better with the poor old woman than with the horse's legs.

"That was ill done, and I say it," said our Lord.

"Oh! for that matter," said the Smith, "there's not many who'll ask after her, I'll be bound; but it's a shame of the Devil, if this is the way he holds to what is written up over the door."

"If you might have three wishes from me," said our Lord, "what would you wish for?"

"Only try me," said the Smith, "and you'll soon know."

So our Lord gave him three wishes.

"Well," said the Smith, "first and foremost, I wish that anyone whom I ask to climb up into the pear tree that stands outside by the wall of my forge, may stay sitting there till I ask him to come down again. The second wish I wish is, that anyone whom I ask to sit down in my easy chair which stands inside the workshop yonder, may stay sitting there till I ask him to get up. Last of all, I wish that

anyone whom I ask to creep into the steel purse which I have in my
pocket, may stay in it till I give him leave to creep out again."

"You have wished as a wicked man," said St. Peter; "first and
foremost, you should have wished for God's grace and goodwill."

"I durstn't look so high as that," said the Smith; and after that
our Lord and St. Peter bade him good-bye, and went on their way.

Well, the years went on and on, and when the time was up, the
Devil came to fetch the Smith, as it was written in their bargain.

"Are you ready?" he said, as he stuck his nose in at the door of
the forge.

"Oh," said the Smith, "I must just hammer the head of this ten-
penny nail first; meantime, you can just climb up into the pear tree,

and pluck yourself a pear to gnaw at; you must be both hungry and thirsty after your journey."

So the Devil thanked him for his kind offer, and climbed up into the pear tree.

"Very good," said the Smith; "but now, on thinking the matter over, I find I shall never be able to have done hammering the head of this nail till four years are out at the least. This iron is so plaguy hard; down you can't come in all that time, but may sit up there and rest your bones."

When the Devil heard this, he begged and prayed till his voice was as thin as a silver penny that he might have leave to come down; but there was no help for it. There he was, and there he must stay. At last he had to give his word of honor not to come again till the four years were out, which Smith had spoken of, and then the Smith said, "Very well, now you may come down."

So when the time was up, the Devil came again to fetch the Smith.

"You're ready now, of course," said he; "you've had time enough to hammer the head of that nail, I should think."

"Yes, the head is right enough now," said the Smith; "but still you have come a little tiny bit too soon, for I haven't quite done sharpening the point; such plaguy hard iron I never hammered in all my born days. So while I work at the point, you may just as well sit down in my easy chair and rest yourself; I'll be bound you're weary after coming so far."

"Thank you kindly," said the Devil, and down he plumped into the easy chair; but just as he had made himself comfortable, the Smith said, on second thought, he found he couldn't get the point sharp till four years were out. First of all, the Devil begged so prettily to be let out of the chair, and afterwards, waxing wroth, he began to threaten and scold; but the Smith kept on, all the while excusing

himself, and saying it was all the iron's fault, it was so plaguy hard, and telling the Devil he was not so badly off to have to sit quietly in an easy chair, and that he would let him out to the minute when the four years were over. Well, at last there was no help for it, and the Devil had to give his word of honor not to fetch the Smith till the four years were out; and then the Smith said,

"Well now, you may get up and be off about your business," and away went the Devil as fast as he could lay legs to the ground.

When the four years were over, the Devil came again to fetch the Smith, and he called out, as he stuck his nose in at the door of the forge,

"Now, I know you must be ready."

"Ready, aye, ready," answered the Smith; "we can go now as soon as you please; but hark ye, there is one thing I have stood here and drought, and thought, I would ask you to tell me. Is it true what people say, that the Devil can make himself as small as he pleases?"

"God knows, it is the very truth," said the Devil.

"Oh," said the Smith; "it is true, is it? Then I wish you would just be so good as to creep into this steel purse of mine, and see whether it is sound at the bottom, for to tell you the truth, I'm afraid my travelling money will drop out."

"With all my heart," said the Devil, who made himself small in a trice, and crept into the purse; but he was scarce in when the Smith snapped to the clasp.

"Yes," called out the Devil inside the purse; "it's right and tight everywhere."

"Very good," said the Smith; "I'm glad to hear you say so, but 'more haste the worse speed,' says the old saw, and 'forewarned is forearmed,' says another; so I'll just weld these links a little together, just for safety's sake"; and with that he laid the purse in the furnace, and made it red-hot.

"Au! Au!" screamed the Devil. "Are you mad? Don't you know I'm inside the purse?"

"Yes, I do!" said the Smith; "but I can't help you, for another old saw says, 'one must strike while the iron is hot'"; and as he said this, he took up his sledge hammer, laid the purse on the anvil, and let fly at it as hard as he could.

"Au! Au! Au!" bellowed the Devil, inside the purse.

"Dear Friend, do let me out, and I'll never come near you again."

"Very well!" said the Smith; "now I think the links are pretty well welded, and you may come out"; so he unclasped the purse, and away went the Devil in such a hurry that he didn't once look behind him.

Now, some time after, it came across the Smith's mind that he had done a silly thing in making the Devil his enemy, for, he said to himself,

"If, as is like enough, they won't have me in the Kingdom of Heaven, I shall be in danger of being houseless, since I've fallen out with him who rules over Hell."

So he made up his mind it would be best to try to get either into Hell or Heaven, and to try at once, rather than to put it off any longer, so that he might know how things really stood. Then he threw his sledge hammer over his shoulder and set off; and when he had gone a good bit of the way, he came to a place where two roads met, and where the path to the Kingdom of Heaven parts from the path that leads to Hell, and here he overtook a tailor, who was pelting along with his goose in his hand.

"Good day," said the Smith; "whither are you off to?"

"To the Kingdom of Heaven," said the Tailor, "if I can only get into it. But whither are you going yourself?"

"Oh, our ways don't run together," said the Smith; "for I have made up my mind to try first in Hell, as the Devil and I know something of one another, from old times."

So they bade one another good-bye, and each went his way; but the Smith was a stout, strong man, and got over the ground far faster than the tailor, and so it wasn't long before he stood at the gates of Hell. Then he called the watch, and bade him go and tell the Devil there was someone outside who wished to speak a word with him.

"Go out," said the Devil to the watch, "and ask him who he is." So that when the watch came and told him that, the Smith answered,

"Go and greet the Devil in my name, and say it is the Smith who owns the purse he wots of; and beg him prettily to let me in at once, for I worked at my forge till noon, and I have had a long walk since."

But when the Devil heard who it was, he charged the watch to go back and lock up all the nine locks on the gates of Hell.

"And, besides," he said, "you may as well put on a padlock, for if he only once gets in, he'll turn Hell topsy-turvy!"

Well! said the Smith to himself, when he saw them busy bolting up the gates, "there's no lodging to be got here, that is plain; so I may as well try my luck in the Kingdom of Heaven; and with that he turned round and went back till he reached the crossroads, and then he went along the path the tailor had taken. And now, as he was cross at having gone backwards and forwards so far for no good, he strode along with all his might, and reached the gate of Heaven just as St. Peter was opening it a very little, just enough to let the half-starved tailor slip in. The Smith was still six or seven strides off the gate, so he thought to himself, "Now there's no time to be lost; and, grasping his sledge hammer, he hurled it into the opening of the door just as the tailor slunk in; and if the Smith didn't get in then, when the door was ajar, why I don't know what has become of him.

GERTRUDE'S BIRD

* * *

IN those days when our Lord and St. Peter wandered upon earth, they came once to an old wife's house, who sat baking.

Her name was Gertrude, and she had a red mutch on her head. They had walked a long way, and were both hungry, and our Lord begged hard for a bannock to stay their hunger. Yes, they should have it. So she took a little tiny piece of dough and rolled it out, but as she rolled it, it grew and grew till it covered the whole griddle.

Nay, that was too big; they couldn't have that. So she took a tinier bit still; but when that was rolled out, it covered the whole griddle just the same, and that bannock was too big, she said; they couldn't have that either.

The third time she took a still tinier bit—so tiny you could scarce see it; but it was the same story over again—the bannock was too big.

"Well," said Gertrude; "I can't give you anything; you must just go without, for all those bannocks are too big."

Then our Lord waxed wroth and said, "Since you loved me so little as to grudge me a morsel of food, you shall have this punishment—you shall become a bird, and seek your food between bark and bole, and never get a drop to drink save when it rains."

He had scarce said the last word before she was turned into a great black woodpecker, or Gertrude's bird, and flew from her kneading-trough right up the chimney; and till this very day you may see her flying about, with her red mutch on her head, and her body all black, because of the soot in the chimney; and so she hacks and taps away at the trees for her food and whistles when rain is coming, for she is ever athirst, and then she looks for a drop to cool her tongue.

WHY THE SEA IS SALT

* * *

ONCE on a time, but it was a long, long time ago, there were two brothers, one rich and one poor. Now, one Christmas eve, the poor one hadn't so much as a crumb in the house, either of meat or bread, so he went to his brother to ask him for something to keep Christmas with, in God's name. It was not the first time his brother had been forced to help him, and you may fancy he wasn't very glad to see his face, but he said, "If you will do what I ask you to do, I'll give you a whole flitch of bacon."

So the poor brother said he would do anything, and was full of thanks.

"Well, here is the flitch," said the rich brother, "and now go straight to Hell."

"What I have given my word to do, I must stick to," said the other; so he took the flitch and set off. He walked the whole day, and at dusk he came to a place where he saw a very bright light.

"Maybe this is the place," said the man to himself. So he turned aside, and the first thing he saw was an old, old man, with a long white beard, who stood in an outhouse, hewing wood for the Christmas fire.

"Good even," said the man with the flitch.

"The same to you; whither are you going so late?" said the man.

"Oh! I'm going to Hell, if I only knew the right way," answered the poor man.

"Well, you're not far wrong, for this is Hell," said the old man. When you get inside they will be all for buying your flitch, for meat is scarce in Hell; but mind you don't sell it unless you get the hand-quern which stands behind the door for it. When you come out, I'll teach you how to handle the quern, for it is good to grind almost anything."

So the man with the flitch thanked the other for his good advice, and gave a great knock at the Devil's door.

When he got in, everything went just as the old man had said. All the devils, great and small, came swarming up to him like ants round an anthill, and each tried to outbid the other for the flitch.

"Well!" said the man, "by rights, my wife and I ought to have this flitch for our Christmas dinner; but since you have all set your hearts on it, I suppose I must give it up to you. But if I sell it at all, I'll have for it that quern behind the door yonder."

At first the Devil wouldn't hear of such a bargain, and chaffered and haggled with the man; but he stuck to what he said, and at last the Devil had to part with his quern. When the man got out into the yard, he asked the old woodcutter how he was to handle the quern; and after he had learned how to use it, he thanked the old man and went off home as fast as he could, but still the clock had struck twelve on Christmas ever before he reached his own door.

"Wherever in the world have you been?" said his wife, "Here have I sat hour after hour waiting and watching, without so much as two sticks to lay together under the Christmas brose."

"Oh!" said the man, "I couldn't get back before, for I had to go a long way first for one thing, and then for another; but now you shall see what you shall see."

So he put the quern on the table, and bade it first of all grind lights, then a tablecloth, then meat, then ale, and so on till they had got everything that was nice for Christmas fare. He had only to speak the word, and the quern ground out what he wanted. The wife stood by blessing her stars, and kept on asking where he had got this wonderful quern, but he wouldn't tell her.

"It's all one where I got it from; you see the quern is a good one, and the millstream never freezes, that's enough."

So he ground meat and drink and dainties enough to last out till Twelfth Day, and on the third day he asked all his friends and kin to his house, and gave a great feast. Now, when his rich brother saw all that was on the table, and that was behind in the larder, he grew quite spiteful and wild, for he couldn't bear that his brother should have anything.

"'Twas only on Christmas eve," he said to the rest, "he was in such straits, that he came and asked for a morsel of food in God's name, and now he gives a feast as if he were count or king"; and he turned to his brother and said,

"But whence, in Hell's name, have you got all this wealth?"

"From behind the door," answered the owner of the quern, for he didn't care to let the cat out of the bag. But later on in the evening, when he had had a drop too much, he could keep his secret no longer, and brought out the quern and said,

"There, you see what has gotten me all this wealth"; and so he made the quern grind all kinds of things. When his brother saw it, he set his heart on having the quern, and, after a deal of coaxing, he got it. But he had to pay three hundred dollars for it, and his brother bargained to keep it till hay-harvest, for he thought, if I keep it till then, I can make it grind meat and drink that will last for years. So you may fancy the quern didn't grow rusty for want of work, and when hay-harvest came, the rich brother got it, but the other took care not to teach him how to handle it.

It was evening when the rich brother got the quern home, and next morning he told his wife to go out into the hay-field and toss, while the mowers cut the grass, and he would stay at home and get the dinner ready. So, when dinnertime drew near, he put the quern on the kitchen table and said,

"Grind herrings and milkpap, and grind them good and fast."

So the quern began to grind herrings and milkpap; first of all, all the dishes full, then all the tubs full, and so on till the kitchen floor was quite covered. Then the man twisted and twirled at the quern to get it to stop, but for all his twisting and fingering the quern went on grinding, and in a little while the pap rose so high that the man was like to drown. So he threw open the kitchen door and ran into the parlor, but it wasn't long before the quern had ground the parlor full too, and it was only at the risk of his life that the man could get hold of the latch of the house door through the stream of pap. When he got the door open, he ran out and set off down the road, with the stream of herrings and pap at his heels, roaring like a waterfall over the whole farm.

Now, his wife, who was in the field tossing hay, drought it a long time to dinner, and at last she said—

"Well! though the master doesn't call us home, we may as well go. Maybe he finds it hard work to boil the pap, and will be glad of my help."

The men were willing enough, so they sauntered homewards; but just as they had got a little way up the hill, what should they meet but herrings, and pap, and bread, all running and dashing, and splashing together in a stream, and the master himself, running before them for his life, and as he passed them he bawled out, "Would to heaven each of you had a hundred throats!—but take care you're not drowned in the pap."

Away he went, as though the Evil One were at his heels, to his brother's house, and begged him for God's sake to take back the quern that instant; for, said he—

"If it grinds only one hour more, the whole parish will be swallowed up by herrings and pap."

But his brother wouldn't hear of taking it back till the other paid him down three hundred dollars more.

So the poor brother got both the money and the quern, and it wasn't long before he set up a farmhouse far finer than the one in which his brother lived, and with the quern he ground so much gold that he covered it with plates of gold. And as the farm lay by the seaside, the golden house gleamed and glistened far away over the sea. All who sailed by put ashore to see the rich man in the golden house, and to see the wonderful quern, the fame of which spread far and wide, till there was nobody who hadn't heard tell of it.

So one day there came a skipper who wanted to see the quern; and the first thing he asked was if it could grind salt.

"Grind salt!" said the owner; "I should just think it could. It can grind anything."

When the skipper heard that, he said he must have the quern, cost what it would; for if he only had it, he thought he should be rid of his long voyages across stormy seas for a lading of salt. Well, at first the man wouldn't hear of parting with the quern; but the skipper begged and prayed so hard, that at last he let him have it, but he had to pay many, many thousand dollars for it. Now, when the skipper had got the quern on his back, he soon made off with it, for he was afraid lest the man should change his mind; so he had no time to ask how to handle the quern, but got on board his ship as fast as he could, and set sail. When he had sailed a good way off, he brought the quern on deck and said—

"Grind salt, and grind both good and fast."

Well, the quern began to grind salt so that it poured out like water; and when the skipper had got the ship full, he wished to stop the quern, but whichever way he turned it, and however much he tried, it was no good; the quern kept grinding on, and the heap of salt grew higher and higher, and at last down sunk the ship.

There lies the quern at the bottom of the sea, grinding away at this very day, and that's why the sea is salt.

BUTTERCUP

* * *

ONCE on a time there was a wife who sat and baked. Now, you must know that this woman had a little son, who was so plump and fat, and so fond of good things, that they called him Buttercup; she had a dog, too, whose name was Goldtooth, and as she was baking, all at once Goldtooth began to bark.

"Run out, Buttercup, there's a dear!" said the wife, "and see what Goldtooth is barking at."

So the boy ran out, and came back crying out,

"Oh, God save me. Here comes a great big witch, with her head under her arm, and a bag at her back."

"Jump under the kneading-trough and hide yourself," said his mother.

So in came the old hag!

"Good day!" said she.

"God bless you!" said Buttercup's mother.

"Isn't your Buttercup at home today?" asked the hag.

"No, that he isn't. He's out in the wood with his father, shooting ptarmigan."

"Plague take it," said the hag, "for I had such a nice little silver knife I wanted to give him."

"Pip, pip! here I am," said Buttercup under the kneading-trough, and out he came.

"I'm so old and stiff in the back," said the hag, "you must creep into the bag and fetch it out for yourself."

But when Buttercup was well into the bag, the hag threw it over her back and strode off, and when they had gone a good bit of the way, the old hag got tired, and asked,

"How far is it off to Snoring?"

"Half a mile," answered Buttercup.

So the hag put down the sack on the road, and went aside by herself into the wood, and lay down to sleep. Meantime Buttercup set to work and cut a hole in the sack with his knife; then he crept out and put a great root of a fir tree into the sack, and ran home to his mother.

When the hag got home and saw what there was in the sack, you may fancy she was in a fine rage.

Next day the wife sat and baked again, and her dog began to bark just as he did the day before.

"Run out, Buttercup, my boy," said she, "and see what Goldtooth is barking at."

"Well, I never!" cried Buttercup, as soon as he got out; "if there isn't that ugly old beast coming again with her head under her arm, and a great sack at her back."

"Under the kneading-trough with you and hide," said his mother.

"Good day!" said the hag; "is your Buttercup at home today?"

"I'm sorry to say he isn't," said his mother; "he's out in the wood with his father shooting ptarmigan."

"What a bore," said the hag; "here I have a beautiful little silver spoon I want to give him."

"Pip, pip! here I am," said Buttercup, and crept out.

"I'm so stiff in the back," said the old witch, "you must creep into the sack and fetch it out for yourself."

So when Buttercup was well into the sack, the hag swung it over her shoulders, and set off home as fast as her legs could carry her. But when they had gone a good bit, she grew weary, and asked,

"How far is it off to Snoring?"

"A mile and a half," answered Buttercup.

So the hag set down the sack, and went aside into the wood to sleep a bit, but while she slept, Buttercup made a hole in the sack and got out, and put a great stone into it. Now, when the old witch got home, she made a great fire on the hearth, and put a big pot on it, and got everything ready to boil Buttercup. But when she took the sack, and thought she was going to turn out Buttercup into the pot, down plumped the stone and made a hole in the bottom of the pot, so that the water ran out and quenched the fire. Then the old hag was in a dreadful rage, and said, "If he makes himself ever so heavy next time, he shan't take me in again."

The third day everything went just as it had gone twice before; Goldtooth began to bark, and Buttercup's mother said to him,

"Do run out and see what our dog is barking at."

So out he went, but he soon came back crying out,

"God save us! Here comes the old hag again with her head under her arm, and a sack at her back."

"Jump under the kneading-trough and hide," said his mother.

"Good day!" said the hag, as she came in at the door; "is your Buttercup at home today?"

"You're very kind to ask after him," said his mother; "but he's out in the wood with his father shooting ptarmigan."

"What a bore now," said the old hag; "here have I got such a beautiful little silver fork for him."

"Pip, pip! here I am," said Buttercup, as he came out from under the kneading-trough.

"I'm so stiff in the back," said the hag, "you must creep into the sack and fetch it out for yourself."

But when Buttercup was well inside the sack, the old hag swung it across her shoulders, and set off as fast as she could. This time she did not turn aside to sleep by the way, but went straight home with Buttercup in the sack, and when she reached her house it was Sunday.

So the old hag said to her daughter,

"Now you must take Buttercup and kill him, and boil him nicely till I come back, for I'm off to church to bid my guests to dinner."

So, when all in the house were gone to church, the daughter was to take Buttercup and kill him, but then she didn't know how to set about it at all.

"Stop a bit," said Buttercup; "I'll soon show you how to do it; just lay your head on the chopping block, and you'll soon see."

So the poor silly thing laid her head down, and Buttercup took an axe and chopped her head off, just as if she had been a chicken. Then he laid her head in the bed, and popped her body into the pot, and boiled it so nicely; and when he had done that, he climbed up on the roof, and dragged up with him the fir tree root and the stone, and put the one over the door, and the other at the top of the chimney.

So when the household came back from church, and saw the head on the bed, they thought it was the daughter who lay there asleep; and then they thought they would just taste the broth.

"Good, by my troth!
Buttercup broth,"

said the old hag.

"Good, by my troth!
Daughter broth,"

said Buttercup down the chimney, but no one heeded him.

So the old hag's husband, who was every bit as bad as she, took the spoon to have a taste.

"Good, by my troth!
Buttercup broth,"

said he.

"Good, by my troth!
Daughter broth,"

said Buttercup down the chimney pipe.

Then they all began to wonder who it could be that chattered so, and ran out to see. But when they came out at the door, Buttercup threw down on them the fir tree root and the stone, and broke all their heads to bits. After that he took all the gold and silver that lay in the house, and went home to his mother, and became a rich man.

HERDING THE KING'S HARES

* * *

ONCE there was a farmer who had turned over his farm to his oldest son. But he had three more sons. Their names were Per, Paal, and Espen Ashlad. They stayed at home with their father and wouldn't do a thing, for they fared too well. And they thought themselves too good for anything, and nothing was good enough for them.

But then, at long last, it came to Per's ears that the King wanted a shepherd to herd his hares, and so he told his father that that was where he wanted to go, that was just the thing for him. He would serve no less a man than the King himself. The old man thought there might be some work that would suit him better. The one who was to herd hares had to be lithe and light on his feet and no sleepy-head, for, when the hares began to gad and scud, it would be quite another dance than pottering around the farmyard.

Well, that couldn't be helped. Per would go there and he must go there. So he put his knapsack on his back and trudged down the hill, and when he had walked far, and farther than far, he came to an old woman whose nose had got caught in a log of wood. And when he saw how she pulled and tore to get loose, he began to roar with laughter.

"Don't stand there grinning," said the old woman, "but come

and help a poor body. I was going to chop up some firewood when my nose got caught in a crack, and so I have been standing here, pulling and jerking, and haven't tasted a bit of food for a hundred years," she said.

But Per just laughed still more. He thought it only funny.

If she had been standing like that for a hundred years, she could certainly bear it for another hundred, he said.

When he came to the King's farm, he at once got the job as shepherd. It wasn't hard to get work there. Good food and good pay he should have, and perhaps he would even get the King's daughter in the bargain. But if as much as one of the King's hares got lost, the King would cut three red strips off his back, and throw him into the snake pit.

Well, as long as Per stayed in the lane between the fields and in the cattle run, the hares stayed all in one flock. But as the day went on and they came up into the woods, the hares began to scamper and gad about all over the hills. Per hurried after them. As long as there was one in sight he ran for all he was worth. When the last one had disappeared and he had almost raced himself to death, he saw no more of them. Late in the afternoon he began to stroll homewards, and stopped at the pasture gate, gaping and gazing around for the hares. But no, there didn't come as much as a single hare, and when he got to the King's hall in the evening, the King was standing with his knife ready, and cut three red strips from his back, sprinkled salt and pepper on it, and then into the snake pit with him.

After a while Paal was the one who wanted to set off and herd the King's hares. The old man said the same to him, and even a little more than that. But he would go and he must go, it just couldn't be helped. And it went neither better nor worse with him than it had gone with Per.

The old woman was standing there pulling and jerking with her nose caught in the log, and he laughed and thought it only funny and let her stay there and wriggle.

Work he got on the spot; he didn't get no for an answer. But the hares scudded and scattered all over the hills. It didn't help at bit that he ran for all he was worth in the broiling sun, till he puffed and panted like a shepherd's dog. And when he came home to the King's hall in the evening without a hare, the King was standing there in the courtyard with his knife ready, and cut three strips from his back, sprinkled it with salt and pepper, and then into the snake pit with him.

By and by Espen Ashlad wanted to be off and herd the King's hares, and told the old man about it. He thought it would be just the right kind of work for him to slip around in the woods and fields and strawberry grounds, and to ramble about after a flock of hares, and to take naps on the sunny hillsides in between, he said.

The old man thought there might be some other kind work that would suit him better, for if he didn't fare worse, he certainly wouldn't fare better than his brothers. The one who was to herd the King's hares mustn't stump about like a sleepyhead with leaden socks on his feet, or like a louse on a tarstick; for when the hares began to gad about on the sunny hillsides, it would be at least as bad as trying to catch fleas with mittens on. The one who was to get away from that with a whole back had to be more than lithe and light on his feet; and leap and run he must, faster than a dried skin or a bird's wing.

Well, that couldn't be helped, said Espen Ashlad, he would go to the King's farm to serve the King, for no lesser man would he serve, he said. And the hares he would certainly know how to herd, they couldn't be so much worse than the goat and the calf.

Then the Ashlad put his knapsack on his back and trudged down the hill. When he had gone far, and farther than far, so that he began to get good and hungry, he came to the old woman who was standing with her nose in the log of wood, pulling and jerking and trying to get loose.

"Good day, Granny," he said. "Are you standing here sharpening your nose, you poor old soul?"

"Oh, but nobody has called me Granny for a hundred years," said the old woman. "Come now and help me to get loose and give me something to eat, for I have had no food in my mouth during all that time, and I'll do you a good turn again for that," she said.

Yes, then she might well need both food and drink, said Espen Ashlad.

Then he split the log for her so she got her nose out of the crack, and he shared his food with her, and they sat down to eat. The old woman had no lack of appetite, you may be sure, so she took the lion's share of the food.

When they had finished, she gave the Ashlad a whistle and told him how to use it. If he blew it from one end, the things which he wanted to get rid of would scatter to all sides, and when he blew it from the other end, they would all come back again. If the whistle was lost or was taken from him, he had only to wish for it and it would come back to him.

"That was some whistle," thought Espen Ashlad.

When he came to the King's farm, he at once was hired as a shepherd. It wasn't hard to get work there, and food and good pay he should have. And if he was able to herd the King's hares so not one was lost, he might perhaps even get the King's daughter. But if any got away, even one of the tiniest hares, they were to cut three red strips from his back, and the King was so sure of this that he went straight over and sharpened his knife then and there.

"It will be easy enough to herd these hares," thought Espen Ashlad, for when they were out of the stable they were almost as tame as a flock of sheep, and as long as they stayed in the lane between the fields and in the cattle run, he had them all in a flock. But when they reached the woody slope towards noontime, and the sun began to glare and broil on clearings and slopes, they began to scatter and gad about all over the hills.

"Hey! hey! Off you go," cried Espen Ashlad, and blew the whistle from one end, and off they went to all the corners of the world, and out of sight. But when he came to a green glade where once there had been a charcoal kiln, he blew the whistle from the other end, and in the jerk of a lamb's tail all the hares were back and stood lined up in rows and ranks, so he could look them over like a troop of soldiers on the drill ground.

"This is some whistle," thought Espen.

Then he went to sleep on a sunny hillside, and the hares scudded about and took care of themselves. Towards evening he whistled them together again and led them back to the King's hall just like a flock of sheep.

The King and the Queen and the Princess, too, stood in the doorway and wondered what kind of a fellow this might be, who could herd the hares so well that he brought them home again.

The King counted and counted the hares, and pointed with his finger and counted again, but there wasn't so much as a leveret missing.

"What a boy!" said the Princess.

The next day he went to the woods to herd again. But as he was lazing about in the strawberry field, up came the chambermaid of the King's hall. She was to try to find out how it happened that he could herd the King's hares so well.

Well, he pulled out the whistle and showed it to her, and then he blew into one end so the hares scattered like the wind over hills and dales, and then he blew into the other end and the hares came trotting back to the strawberry field and lined up there in rows and ranks again.

That was a strange whistle, said the maid, and she would pay him one hundred dollars for it, if he would sell it, she said.

"Oh, yes, it is some whistle," said Espen Ashlad. It wasn't for sale for money, but if she would give him two hundred dollars and a kiss for each dollar, then she could have it, he said.

Oh, yes, that she would gladly do, she would willingly give him two for each one, and many thanks in the bargain.

So she got the whistle; but when she arrived at the King's hall the whistle had gone, for Espen Ashlad had wished it back again. And towards evening he came home with his hares again; they trotted along like a flock of sheep, and for all that the King counted and pointed, it didn't help. He could not find so much as a hair of them missing.

The third day he was out herding, they sent the Princess out to try to get the whistle away from him. She made herself as sweet as sugar and as gay as a lark, and then she offered him two hundred dollars if he would sell her the whistle and tell her how to behave to get it safe home.

"Yes, it certainly is some whistle," said Espen Ashlad, and it wasn't for sale, he said. But if that was all the same, he would have to sell it for her sake. If she would give him the two hundred dollars and a kiss in the bargain for each dollar, then she could have the whistle. And if she wanted to keep it, she had to watch it well—that was her business.

That was a high price for a hare-whistle, thought the Princess, and it went a little against the grain to give him the kisses. But as they were in the wood so nobody could either see or hear it, she would have to let it go, for the whistle she must have, she said. And when Espen Ashlad had got what he was to have, she got the whistle, and she kept it tightly pressed in her hand all the way home. But when she arrived at the hall and wanted to show it, it had vanished from between her fingers.

The next day the Queen would go herself and try to get the whistle from him, and she was quite sure she would bring it back with her too.

She was more stingy with the dollars, and didn't offer him more than fifty, but she had to raise her price till at last it was three hundred. Espen Ashlad said it was some whistle and that it was a ridiculous bid. But for her sake he had to let it pass; if she would give him three hundred dollars and a smacking kiss for each dollar, she could have it. Of that he got full measure, for she wasn't stingy in that.

When she had got the whistle, she tied it on to her and hid it too. But she had no better luck than the others, for when she wanted to pull it out and show it, the whistle had vanished. And in the evening Espen Ashlad came home driving his hares like a flock of tame sheep.

"Oh, you are no good, any of you," said the King. "I'll have to go myself if we are to get this confounded whistle away from him."

So when Espen Ashlad had gone to the woods with the hares the next day, the King set out after him and caught up with him on the same sunny hillside where the women folk had made their bargains with him. Yes, they were great friends and agreed about everything, and Espen showed him the whistle and let him hold it, and blew it, first in one end and then in the other. And the King thought it a very strange whistle and wanted by all means to buy it.

"Yes, it certainly is some whistle," said Espen Ashlad, "but it isn't for sale for money. But do you see the white mare that stands there in the bog beside the great fir tree?" he said.

"Yes, that is my own horse, that is Whitey," said the King. He knew that himself without anybody telling him.

"Well, if you'll give me a thousand dollars and kiss Whitey, you shall have the whistle."

"Isn't it for sale at any other price?" asked the King.

"No, it isn't," said Espen Ashlad.

"Well, but I take it that you'll let me put my silk handkerchief between me and the horse?" said the King.

That he might do. And so he got the whistle and put it in his purse, and the purse he put in his pocket, and the pocket he buttoned well. But when he arrived at his house and wanted to pull out the whistle, he was no better off than the women folk. He had no more whistle to show than they had. And Espen Ashlad came driving the hares home and not a hair of them was missing.

The King was in a great rage that the Ashlad had fooled them all and had cheated him, too, out of the whistle. Now the Ashlad should lose his life, there was no question about that. 'Twas always best to get rid of such a rogue, the sooner the better.

Espen Ashlad said this was neither just nor justice, he had only done what they wanted him to do; and so he had saved his back and his life as well as he could. "Well, never mind that," said the King.

"If you can tell so many lies that they fill the big brewing vat so that it overflows, your life shall be spared," he said.

That was neither a hard nor a long task, said Espen Ashlad. He was sure he could do that. And so he began to tell how things had happened right from the beginning. He told about the old woman with her nose in the log of wood, and every now and then he threw in: "I have to think up some lies, if the vat is to get filled." Then he talked about the whistle which he had got, about the chamber-maid who came to him and wanted to buy it for a hundred dollars and about all the kisses she had to give into the bargain, over there on the sunny hillside. And then he talked about the Princess, how she came to him and kissed him so well to get the whistle, because nobody could see or hear it over there in the woods. "I have to tell a lot of lies, if the vat is to get filled," said Espen Ashlad. Then he talked about the Queen, how stingy she was with her dollars and how generous she was with her smacks. "I have to tell a lot of lies, if the vat is to get filled," said Espen Ashlad.

"I think it's getting pretty full now," said the King.

"Oh, no," said the Queen.

Then he began to talk about the King who came to him, and about the white mare down in the bog, and how if he wanted the whistle he had to—he had to—

"Yes, with your permission I have to tell a whole lot of lies, if the vat is to get filled," said Espen Ashlad.

"Wait, wait. It is filled, lad. Don't you see it is flowing over?" cried the King.

Then the King and Queen thought it best to give him the Princess and half the kingdom; it just couldn't be helped.

"That certainly was some whistle," said Espen Ashlad.

THE ASHLAD WHO MADE
THE PRINCESS SAY, "YOU LIE"

* ** ** *

ONCE on a time there was a king who had a daughter, and she was such a dreadful story teller that the like of her was not to be found far or near. So the King gave out, that if anyone could tell such a string of lies as would get her to say, "You lie," he should have her to wife, and half the kingdom besides. Well, many came, as you may fancy, to try their luck, for everyone would have been very glad to have the Princess, to say nothing of the kingdom; but they all cut a sorry figure, for the Princess was so given to story telling, that all their lies went in at one ear and out of the other. Among the rest came three brothers to try their luck, and the two elder went first, but they fared no better than those who had gone before them. Last of all the third, the Ashlad, set off and found the Princess in the farmyard.

"Good morning," he said, "glad to meet you again." "Good morning," said she, "and the same to you." Then she went on—

"You haven't such a fine farmyard as ours, I'll be bound; for when two shepherds stand, one at each end of it, and blow their ram's horns, the one can't hear the other."

"Haven't we though!" answered the Ashlad; "ours is far bigger; for when a cow begins to go with calf at one end of it, she doesn't get to the other end before the time to drop her calf is come."

"I dare say!" said the Princess. "Well, but you haven't such a big ox, after all, as ours yonder; for when two herdboys sit, one on each horn, they can't touch each other with a twenty-foot rule."

"Stuff!" said the Ashlad; "is that all? Why, we have an ox who is so big, that when two men sit, one on each horn, and each blows his great hunting-horn, they can't hear one another."

"I dare say!" said the Princess. "But you haven't so much milk as we, I'll be bound; for we milk our kine into great pails, and carry them indoors, and empty them into great tubs, and so we make great, great cheeses."

"Well," said the Ashlad. "We milk ours into great tubs, and then we put them in carts and drive them indoors, and then we turn them out into great brewing vats, and so we make cheeses as big as a great house. We had, too, a dun mare to tread the cheese well together when it was making; but once she tumbled down into the cheese, and we lost her; and after we had eaten at this cheese seven years, we came upon a great dun mare, alive and kicking. Well, once after that I was going to drive this mare to the mill, and her backbone snapped in two. But I wasn't put out, not I, for I took a spruce sapling, and put it into her for a backbone and she had no other backbone all the while we had her. But the sapling grew up into such a tall tree, that I climbed right up to heaven by it, and when I got there, I saw the Virgin Mary sitting and spinning the foam of the sea into pig's-bristle ropes. But just then the spruce-fir broke short off, and I couldn't get down again, so the Virgin Mary let me down by one of the ropes, and down I slipped straight into a fox's hole, and who should sit there but my mother and your father cobbling shoes; and just as I stepped in, my mother gave your father such a box on the head, that the scab dropped from his scurvy pate."

"You lie!" said the Princess. "My father never in his life had a scurvy head."

So the Ashlad got the Princess to wife, and half the kingdom besides.

WELL DONE AND ILL PAID

* * *

ONCE on a time there was a man, who had to drive his sledge to the wood for fuel. So a bear met him.

"Out with your horse," said the bear, "or I'll strike all your sheep dead by summer."

"Oh! heaven help me then," said the man; "there's not a stick of firewood in the house; you must let me drive home a load of fuel, else we shall be frozen to death. I'll bring the horse to you tomorrow morning."

Yes! on those terms he might drive the wood home; that was a bargain. But Bruin said, if he didn't come back, he should lose all his sheep by summer.

So the man got the wood on the sledge and rattled home-wards, but he wasn't overpleased at the bargain, you may fancy. So just then a fox met him.

"Why, what's the matter?" said the fox. "Why are you so down in the mouth?"

"Oh, if you want to know," said the man, "I met a bear up yonder in the wood, and I had to give my word to him to bring Dobbin back tomorrow, at this very hour; for if he didn't get him, he said he would tear all my sheep to death by summer."

"Stuff, nothing worse than that?" said the fox. "If you'll give me your fattest wether I'll soon set you free; see if I don't."

Yes! the man gave his word, and swore he would keep it too.

"Well, when you come with Dobbin tomorrow for the bear," said the fox, "I'll make a clatter up in that scree, and when the bear asks what that noise is, you must say 'tis Peter the Marksman, who is the best shot in the world; and after that you must help yourself."

Next day off set the man, and when he met the bear, something began to make a clatter up in the scree.

"Hist! what's that?" said the bear.

"Oh! that's Peter the Marksman, to be sure," said the man.

"He's the best shot in the world. I know him by his voice."

"Have you seen any bears about here, Eric?" shouted out a voice in the wood.

"Say, no!" said the bear.

"No, I haven't seen any," said Eric.

"What's that then, that stands alongside your sledge?" called out the voice in the wood.

"Say it's an old fir-stump," said the bear.

"Oh, it's only an old fir-stump," said the man.

"Such fir-stumps we take in our country and roll them on our sledges," called out the voice. "If you can't do it yourself, I'll come and help you."

"Say you can help yourself, and roll me up on the sledge," said the bear.

"No, thank ye, I can help myself well enough," said the man, and rolled the bear on to the sledge.

"Such fir-stumps we always bind fast on our sledges in our part of the world," called out the voice. "Shall I come and help you?"

"Say you can help yourself, and bind me fast, do," said the bear.

"No, thanks, I can help myself well enough," said the man, who set to binding Bruin fast with all the ropes he had, so that at last the bear couldn't stir a paw.

"Such fir-stumps we always drive our axes into in our part of the world," called out the voice; "for then we guide them better going down the steep pitches."

"Pretend to drive your axe into me, do now," said the bear.

Then the man took up his axe, and at one blow split the bear's skull, so that Bruin lay dead in a trice, and so the man and the fox were great friends, and on the best terms.

But when they came near the farm, the fox said,

"I've no mind to go right home with you, for I can't say I like your tykes; so I'll just wait here, and you can bring the wether to me. But mind and pick out one nice and fat."

Yes! the man would be sure to do that, and thanked the fox much for his help. So when he had put up Dobbin, he went across to the sheep-stall.

"Whither away, now?" asked his old dame.

"Oh!" said the man, "I'm only going to the sheep-stall to fetch a fat wether for that cunning fox, who set our Dobbin free. I gave him my word I would."

"Wether, indeed," said the old dame; "never a one shall that thief of a fox get. Haven't we got Dobbin safe, and the bear into the bargain? And as for the fox, I'll be bound he's stolen more of our geese than the wether is worth; and even if he hasn't stolen them, he will. No, no; take a brace of your swiftest hounds in a sack, and slip them loose after him; and then, perhaps, we shall be rid of this robbing Reynard."

Well, the man thought that good advice; so he took two fleet red hounds, put them into a sack, and set off with them.

"Have you brought the wether?" said the fox.

"Yes, come and take it," said the man as he untied the sack and let slip the hounds.

"HUF," said the fox, and gave a great spring. "True it is what the old saw says, 'Well done is often ill paid'; and now, too, I see the truth of another saying, 'Nothing as unkind as one's own kind.'" That was what the fox said as he ran off, and saw the red foxy hounds at his heels.

WHY THE BEAR
IS STUMPY-TAILED

* * *

ONE day the bear met the fox, who came slinking along with a string of fish he had stolen.

"Whence did you get those from?" asked the bear.

"Oh! my Lord Bruin, I've been out fishing and caught them," said the fox.

So the bear had a mind to learn to fish too, and bade the fox tell him how he was to set about it.

"Oh, it's an easy craft for you," answered the fox, "and soon learned. You've only got to go upon the ice, and cut a hole and stick your tail down into it; and so you must go on holding it there as long as you can. You're not to mind if your tail smarts a little; that's when the fish bite. The longer you hold it there the more fish you'll get; and then all at once out with it, with a cross pull sideways, and with a strong pull too."

Yes; the bear did as the fox had said, and held his tail a long, long time down in the hole, till it was fast frozen in. Then he pulled it out with a cross pull, and it snapped off short. That's why Bruin goes about with a stumpy tail this very day.

THE FOX AS HERDSMAN

 * * *

ONCE on a time there was a woman who went out to hire a herdsman, and she met a bear.

"Whither away, Goody?" said Bruin.

"Oh, I'm going out to hire a herdsman," answered the woman.

"Why not have me for a herdsman?" said Bruin.

"Well, why not?" said the woman. "If you only knew how to
call the flock; just let me hear."

"Ow, Ow!" growled the bear.

"No, no! I won't have you," said the woman, as soon as she heard
him say that, and off she went on her way.

So, when she had gone a bit further, she met a wolf.

"Whither away, Goody?" asked the wolf.

"Oh!" said she, "I'm going out to hire a herdsman." "Why not
have me for a herdsman?" said the wolf.

"Well, why not? If you can only call the flock; let me hear," said
she.

"UH, UH!" said the wolf.

"No, no!" said the woman; "you'll never do for me."

Well, after she had gone a while longer, she met a fox.

"Whither away, Goody?" asked the fox.

"Oh, I'm just going out to hire a herdsman," said the woman.

"Why not have me for your herdsman?" asked the fox.

"Well, why not?" said she; "if you only knew how to call the flock; let me hear."

"Dil-Dal-Holom," sung out the fox, in such a fine clear voice.

"Yes; I'll have you for my herdsman," said the woman; and so she set the fox to herd her flock.

The first day the fox was herdsman he ate up all the woman's goats; the next day he made an end of all her sheep; and the third day he ate up all her kine. So, when he came home at even, the woman asked what he had done with all her flocks.

"Oh!" said the fox, "their skulls are in the stream, and their bodies in the holt."

Now, Goody stood and churned when the fox said this, but she thought she might as well step out and see after her flock; and while she was away the fox crept into the churn and ate up the cream. So when Goody came back and saw that, she fell into such a rage, that she snatched up the little morsel of the cream that was left, and threw it at the fox as he ran off, so that he got a dab of it on the end of his tail, and that's the reason why the fox has a white tip to his brush.

GUDBRAND ON
THE HILLSIDE

* * *

ONCE on a time there was a man whose name was Gudbrand. He had a farm which lay far, far away upon a hillside, and so they called him Gudbrand on the Hillside.

Now, you must know this man and his good wife lived so happily together, and understood one another so well, that all the husband did the wife thought so well done there was nothing like it in the world, and she was always glad whatever he turned his hand to. The farm was their own land, and they had a hundred dollars lying at the bottom of their chest, and two cows tethered up in a stall in their farmyard.

So one day his wife said to Gudbrand,

"Do you know, dear, I think we ought to take one of our cows into town and sell it; that's what I think. Then we shall have some money in hand, and such well-to-do people as we ought to have ready money like the rest of the world. As for the hundred dollars at the bottom of the chest yonder, we can't make a hole in them, and I'm sure I don't know what we want with more than one cow. Besides, we shall gain a little in another way, for then I shall get off with only looking after one cow, instead of having, as now, to feed and litter and water, two."

Well, Gudbrand thought his wife talked right good sense, so he set off at once with the cow on his way to town to sell her. But when he got to the town, there was no one who would buy his cow.

"Well! well! never mind," said Gudbrand; "at the worst, I can only go back home again with my cow. I've both stable and tether for her, I should think, and the road is no farther out than in"; and with that he began to toddle home with his cow.

But when he had gone a bit of the way, a man met him who had a horse to sell, so Gudbrand thought 'twas better to have a horse than a cow, so he swapped with the man. A little farther on he met a man walking along and driving a fat pig before him, and he thought it better to have a fat pig than a horse, so he swapped with the man. After that he went a little farther, and a man met him with a goat; so he thought it better to have a goat than a pig, and he swapped with the man that owned the goat. Then he went on a good bit till he met a man who had a sheep, and he swapped with him too, for he thought it always better to have a sheep than a goat. After a while he met a man with a goose, and he swopped away the sheep for the goose; and when he had walked a long, long time, he met a man with a cock, and he swapped with him, for he thought in this wise, "'Tis surely better to have a cock than a goose." Then he went on till the day was far spent, and he began to get very hungry, so he sold the cock for a shilling, and bought food with the money, for, thought Gudbrand on the Hillside, "'Tis always better to save one's life than to have a cock."

After that he went on home till he reached his nearest neighbor's house, where he turned in.

"Well," said the owner of the house, "how did things go with you in town?"

"Rather so so," said Gudbrand. "I can't praise my luck, nor do I blame it either," and with that he told the whole story from first to last.

"Ah!" said his friend, "you'll get nicely called over the coals, that one can see, when you get home to your wife. Heaven help you, I wouldn't stand in your shoes for anything."

"Well," said Gudbrand on the Hillside, "I think things might have gone much worse with me; but now, whether I have done wrong or not, I have so kind a goodwife, she never has a word to say against anything that I do."

"Oh!" answered his neighbor, "I hear what you say, but I don't believe it for all that."

"Shall we lay a bet upon it?" asked Gudbrand on the Hillside. "I have a hundred dollars at the bottom of my chest at home; will you lay as many against them?"

Yes! the friend was ready to bet. So Gudbrand stayed there till evening, when it began to get dark, and then they went together to his house, and the neighbor was to stand outside the door and listen, while the man went in to see his wife.

"Good evening!" said Gudbrand on the Hillside.

"Good evening!" said the goodwife. "Oh! is that you? Now God be praised."

Yes! it was he. So the wife asked how things had gone with him in town.

"Oh! only so so," answered Gudbrand; "not much to brag of. When I got to town there was no one who would buy the cow, so you must know I swapped it away for a horse."

"For a horse!" said his wife; "well that is good of you. Thanks with all my heart. We are so well-to-do that we may drive to church, just as well as other people, and if we choose to keep a horse we have a right to get one, I should think. So run out, children, and put up the horse."

"Ah!" said Gudbrand, "but you see, I've not got the horse after all; for when I got a bit farther on the road, I swapped it away for a pig."

"Think of that now!" said the wife. "You did just as I should have done myself. A thousand thanks! Now I can have a bit of bacon in the house to set before people when they come to see me, that I can. What do we want with a horse? People would only say we had got so proud that we couldn't walk to church. Go out, children, and put up the pig in the sty."

"But I've not got the pig either," said Gudbrand; "for when I got a little farther on, I swapped it away for a milch goat."

"Bless us!" cried his wife, "how well you manage everything! Now I think it over, what should I do with a pig? People would only point at us and say, 'Yonder they eat up all they have got.' No! now I have got a goat, and I shall have milk and cheese, and keep the goat too. Run out, children, and put up the goat."

"Nay, but I haven't got the goat either," said Gudbrand, "for a little farther on I swapped it away and got a fine sheep instead."

"You don't say so?" cried his wife. "Why, you do everything to please me, just as if I had been with you. What do we want with a goat? If I had it I should lose half my time in climbing up the hills to get it down. No, if I have a sheep, I shall have both wool and clothing, and fresh meat in the house. Run out, children, and put up the sheep."

"But I haven't got the sheep any more than the rest," said Gudbrand; "for when I had gone a bit farther, I swapped it away for a goose."

"Thank you! thank you! With all my heart," cried his wife. "What should I do with a sheep? I have no spinning wheel, nor carding comb, nor should I care to worry myself with cutting, and shaping, and sewing clothes. We can buy clothes now, as we have always done; and now I shall have roast goose, which I have longed so often to taste; and, besides, down to stuff my little pillow with. Run out, children, and put up the goose."

"Ah!" said Gudbrand, "but I haven't the goose either; for when I had gone a bit farther I swapped it away for a cock."

"Dear me!" Cried his wife, how you think of everything! Just as should have done myself. A cock, think of that! Why it's as good as an eight-day clock, for every morning the cock crows at four o'clock, and we shall be able to stir our stumps in good time. What should we do with a goose? I don't know how to cook it; and as for my pillow, I can stuff it with bog-cotton. Run out, children, and put up the cock."

"But, after all, I haven't got the cock," said Gudbrand; "for when I had gone a bit farther I got as hungry as a hunter, so I was forced to sell the cock for a shilling, for fear I should starve."

"Now God be praised for that you did so!" cried his wife.

"Whatever you do, you do it always just after my own heart. What should we do with the cock? We are our own masters, I should think, and can lie abed in the morning as long as we like. Heaven be thanked that I have got you safe back again; you who do everything so well that I want neither cock nor goose; neither pigs nor kine."

Then Gudbrand opened the door and said,

"Well, what do you say now? Have I won the hundred dollars?" and his neighbor was forced to allow that he had.

LITTLE FRIKK AND HIS FIDDLE

* * *

ONCE upon a time there was a poor crofter who had an only son. The boy was puny and of indifferent health, so that he was too frail to go out as a day laborer. He was called Frikk, and since he was also small of stature they called him Little Frikk.

In his home food was scarce, so the father went around the countryside and tried to find somebody who would hire the boy as shepherd or errand boy. But nobody wanted his son, until at last he came to the sheriff: he was willing to take him on, because he had just fired one errand boy, and nobody wanted to hire himself with the sheriff. He was known to be a bad one. Something is better than nothing, the crofter thought; the boy would at least be fed, for with the sheriff he was to serve for his grub only, wages or clothes were not even mentioned. But when the boy had been with the sheriff for three years, he wanted to leave, and then the sheriff paid him full wages in one sum. One penny a year, said the sheriff, it could not be less. So he was given the sum of three pence.

To Little Frikk this seemed a lot of money, as he had never owned so much. But he asked if he was not to have some more.

"I have already given you more than we agreed on," said the sheriff.

"Can't I have something for clothing then?" Little Frikk said. The things I had when I came here I have worn out, and I have nothing in place of them," and now in fact he was so ragged, his tatters just flapped about his body.

"When you have had all we were agreed on, and three pence over, I don't owe you any more," the sheriff said. But he was given leave to go out into the kitchen and get a bit of food to put in his knapsack, and then he started on the way to town, to buy himself some clothes. He was happy and merry, for he had never seen a penny before, and every few moments he had to feel, if he still had the three of them.

When he had walked a long, long way, he came into a narrow valley with high mountains on all sides, so that it seemed to him there could not possibly be a way out. He began to wonder what might be on the other side of these mountains, and how he was to get over them.

But he had to get over them, and so he jogged on. He was not strong and had to rest ever so often, and then he would count how much money he had. When he had arrived on top of the mountains he saw nothing but a wide upland moor. He sat down and was going to look if he had all his pennies, when all of a sudden a beggar stood before him. He was big and tall. The boy screamed, when he saw how big and tall he really was.

"You must not be afraid," said the beggar; "I won't hurt you. I am only asking for a penny, in the name of God."

"So help me," said the boy, "I have no more than three pennies, and I am going to town to buy me some clothes with them."

"I am worse off than you are," said the beggar. "I have no penny at all, and I am even more ragged than you are."

"Well, I'll have to let you have it then," said the boy.

When he had walked on for a while he felt tired and sat down again to rest. When he looked about him, there was another beggar, but he was still bigger and uglier than the first one; and when the boy saw how big and ugly and tall he really was, he screamed.

"Don't be afraid of me, I won't hurt you. I am only asking for a penny, in the name of God," the beggar said.

"So help me," said the boy, "all I have is two pennies and I am going to town to buy some clothes with them. If I had only met you a while..."

"I am worse off than you are," said the beggar, "I have no penny at all, and a bigger body and even less clothes."

"Well, you had better have it then," the boy said.

Then he walked on for a while, until he felt tired, and then he sat down to rest. But no sooner had he sat down, when another beggar came up to him, but he was so big and so ugly and so tall, it seemed to the boy he had to look up, right up into the sky. And when he saw how big and ugly and ragged he was, he screamed.

"Don't be afraid of me, my boy," said the beggar. "I am not going to hurt you; I am only a poor man who is asking for a penny, in the name of God."

"So help me indeed," said Little Frikk, "now all I have left is one penny, and I am going to town to buy some clothes with it. If I had only met you a little while ago..."

"But I have no penny at all, and a bigger body and worse clothes, so I am worse off than you are," said the beggar.

Well, he'd better let him have the penny then, Little Frikk said; it could not be helped, because then each of them had one, even if he himself had nothing.

"Now, because you are so kindhearted, that you were willing to give away all you owned, said the beggar, I'll grant you a wish for each of the pennies"; for it was the same beggar who had received all the pennies—he had only changed his shape each time, so that the boy would not recognize

"I always wanted so to listen to fiddles playing and to see people happy and merry as they danced," said the boy. "So if I may wish for something I really want to have, I would like to have a fiddle like that so that every living thing shall dance to it," he said.

He should have it, but that was a poor wish, said the beggar. "Make better wishes for the other two pennies."

"I always wanted so to go hunting and shooting," said Little Frikk; "so if I may wish for something I really want, I'll wish I had a shotgun which is such that I shall hit whatever I aim at, be it ever so far away."

He should have it, but it was a poor wish, said the beggar. "Make a better wish for the last penny."

"I always wanted so to be among people who were friendly and kindhearted," said little Frikk; "so if I may have what I want, I wish that no one should refuse me the first thing I asked for."

"That wish was not so bad," said the beggar, and with that he hurried away among the hills and disappeared, and the boy laid down to sleep. The next day he walked down from the mountain with his fiddle and his shotgun.

First he went to a storekeeper and asked for clothes, and at a farm he asked for a horse, and at another for a sleigh; and at one place he asked for a lap robe of bearskin; and nowhere did he get no for an answer. If they were ever so miserly they had to give him what he asked for. In the end he travelled through the countryside in state, like a well-to-do person, with his horse and sleigh.

After a while he met the sheriff with whom he had served.

"Good morning, master," said Little Frikk with the Fiddle, as he halted and greeted him.

"Good morning," said the sheriff. "Say, was I ever your master?"

"Why, don't you remember? I served you three years for three pennies," said Little Frikk.

"Goodness me, you've prospered quickly then," said the sheriff. "How did it happen that you have become such a grand person?"

"Oh, it just happened," the little one said.

"And you are so giddy that you travel about with a fiddle?" said the sheriff.

"Oh, yes, I've always wanted so to make people dance, said the boy. "But the most precious thing I have is this shotgun," he said, "for whatever I aim at comes down, even if it is ever so far away. Do you see that magpie sitting in the spruce over there?" said Little Frikk. "What would you bet, I'll get her from here, where we are standing?"

The sheriff was willing to bet his horse and his farm and a hundred dollars, that Frikk could not do that, but in the end they agreed that he was to bet all the money he carried on him.

And he was to go and pick up the magpie if it did fall down, for he would never believe it was possible to hit anything with a shotgun at that distance. But as soon as the gun cracked, the magpie dropped down in a big patch of briars, and the sheriff hurried over to the briars to pick it up and show it to the boy. Just then Little Frikk made the first stroke on his fiddle, and the sheriff danced, and cried, and called out for mercy, until the tatters whipped about him, and he had scarcely a stitch on his body.

"Well, I think now you are about as ragged as I was, when I left your service," said the boy, "so I'll let you off." But first the sheriff had to hand over to him the money he had bet, when he did not believe Frikk could hit the magpie.

When the boy came to town he took lodgings in an inn.

He played, and the people who came there danced, and they lived well and merrily. He had no worries, for nobody could refuse him what he asked for.

But just as they played and had a good time, the watchmen came to drag the boy to the courthouse, for the sheriff had complained and said, he had been waylaid, robbed and almost killed by that boy, and now he was to be hanged, and no pardon. But Little Frikk had means to save himself, and that was his fiddle. He started playing it, and then the watchmen had to dance, till they dropped down, gasping. Then they sent soldiers and guards to take him. But they had no better luck than the watchmen. When Little Frikk took up the fiddle they had to dance as long as he was able to make it sound, but the soldiers tired long before he did.

In the end they sneaked up and took him, whilst he lay sleeping one night, and when they had got hold of him he was sentenced to be hanged, and they carried him off to the gallows without delay. A big crowd gathered to see this prodigy, and the sheriff was also in the crowd, as pleased as punch because he was going to get redress for his money and his hide, and look on, when they hanged him.

But they had to move slowly, for Little Frikk was a poor walker, and he pretended to be even worse, and the fiddle and the shotgun he dragged along with him, nobody was able to get them away from him. And when he came to the gallows and had to mount the ladder, he rested on every rung. On the upmost he sat down and asked, if they could refuse him his last wish,—would they not give him leave to play a tune on his fiddle, he wanted so much to play a dance before they hanged him.—Oh, no, it would be a sin and a shame to refuse him that, they said, they could not say no to anything he asked for. But the sheriff begged them for God's sake not to let him pluck a string, that would be the end of all of them. If the boy was given leave to play, they must tie him to the great birch over there. Little Frikk did not dawdle, he made the fiddle sing out at once, and everybody who was there had to dance, those who walked on two legs as well as those who walk on four. They danced, the parson and the minister, and the judge and the constable, and the sheriff and the hangman, and dogs and pigs. They danced and they laughed and cried all at once, some danced until they dropped down and lay like dead, and some danced until they fell down in a swoon. A bad time they had, all of them, but the worst of it had the sheriff, for he stood tied to the birch and danced, and rubbed big pieces off his backside. It did not occur to anybody to do anything to Little Frikk, and he was free to go about with his fiddle and his shotgun just as he liked, and he lived well and happily all his days, since nobody could say no to the first boon he asked of them.

THE HUSBAND WHO WAS
TO MIND THE HOUSE

* * *

ONCE on a time there was a man, so surly and cross, he never thought his wife did anything right in the house.

So, one evening, in haymaking time, he came home, scolding and swearing, and making a racket.

"Goodness me, don't be so angry, there's a good man," said his wife. "Tomorrow let's change our work, I'll go out with the mowers and mow, and you shall mind the house at home."

Yes! the husband thought that would do very well. He was quite willing, he said.

So, early next morning, his wife took a scythe over her shoulder, and went out into the hay field with the mowers, and began to mow; but the man was to mind the house, and do the work at home.

First of all, he wanted to churn the butter; but when he had churned a while, he got thirsty, and went down to the cellar to tap a pitcher of ale. So, just when he had knocked in the bung, and was putting the tap into the cask, he heard, overhead, the pig come into the kitchen. Off he ran up the cellar steps, with the tap in his hand, as fast as he could, to look after the pig, lest it should upset the churn; but when he got up, and saw the pig had already knocked the churn over, and stood there, routing and grunting amid the cream

which was running all over the floor, he got so wild with rage that
he quite forgot the ale-barrel, and ran at the pig as hard as he could.
He caught it, too, just as it ran out of doors, and gave it such a kick,
that piggy lay dead on the spot. Then all at once he remembered he
had the tap in his hand; but when he got down to the cellar, every
drop of ale had run out of the cask.

Then he went into the dairy and found enough cream left to
fill the churn again, and so he began to churn, for butter they must
have at dinner. When he had churned a bit, he remembered that

their milking cow was still shut up in the byre, and hadn't had a bit to eat or a drop to drink all the morning, though the sun was high. He thought 'twas too far to take her down to the meadow, so he'd just get her up on the house-top for the house, you must know, was thatched with sods, and a fine crop of grass was growing there. Now their house lay close up against a steep down, and he thought if he laid a plank across to the thatch at the back he'd easily get the cow up.

But still he couldn't leave the churn, for there was his little babe crawling about on the floor, and "if I leave it," he thought, the child is sure to upset it." So he took the churn on his back, and went out with it; but he thought he'd better first water the cow before he turned her out on the thatch. So he took up a bucket to draw water out of the well, but, as he stooped down at the well's brink, all the cream ran out of the churn over his shoulders, and so down into the well.

Now it was near dinnertime, and as he hadn't even got the butter yet, he thought he'd best boil the porridge. So he filled the pot with water, and hung it over the fire. When he had done that, he thought the cow might perhaps fall off the thatch and break her legs or her neck. So he got up on the house to tie her up. One end of the rope he made fast to the cow's neck, and the other he slipped down the chimney and tied round his own thigh. He had to make haste, for the water now began to boil in the pot, and he had still to grind the oatmeal.

So he began to grind away; but while he was hard at it, down fell the cow off the housetop after all, and as she fell she dragged the man up the chimney by the rope. There he stuck fast. As for the cow, she hung half way down the wall, swinging between heaven and earth, for she could neither get down nor up.

Now the wife had waited seven lengths and seven breadths for her husband to come and call them home to dinner; but never a call they had; so at last she thought she'd waited long enough, and went home. When she got there and saw the cow hanging in such an ugly place, she ran up and cut the rope in two with her scythe. But as she did this, down came her husband out of the chimney, and when his old dame came to the kitchen, there she found him standing on his head in the porridge pot.

NOT A PIN TO CHOOSE
BETWEEN THEM

* * *

ONCE on a time there was a man, and he had a wife. Now this couple wanted to sow their fields, but they had neither seed-corn nor
money to buy it with. But they had a cow, and the man was to drive
it into town and sell it, to get money to buy corn for seed. But when
it came to the pinch, the wife dared not let her husband start for fear
he should spend the money in drink, so she set off herself with the
cow, and took besides a hen with her.

Close by the town she met a butcher who asked,

"Will you sell that cow, Mistress?"

"Yes, that I will," she answered.

"Well, what do you want for her?"

"Oh! I must have five shillings for the cow, but you shall have
the hen for one hundred dollars."

"Very good!" said the man; "I don't want the hen, and you'll
soon get it off your hands in the town, but I'll give you five shillings
for the cow."

Well, she sold the cow for five shillings, but there was no one in
the town who would give one hundred dollars for a lean, tough old
hen, so she went back to the butcher and said,

"Do all I can, I can't get rid of this hen, master! you must take it too, as you took the cow."

"Well," said the butcher, "come along and we'll see about it." Then he treated her with meat and drink, and gave her so much brandy that she lost her head, and didn't know what she was about, and fell fast asleep. But while she slept, the butcher took and dipped her into a tar barrel, and then laid her down on a heap of feathers. And when she woke up, she was feathered all over, and began to wonder what had befallen her.

Is it me, or is it not me? No, it can never be me; it must be some great strange bird. But what shall I do to find out whether it is me or not. Oh! I know how I shall be able to tell whether it is me. If the calves come and lick me, and our dog Tray doesn't bark at me when I get home, then it must be me, and no one else."

Now, Tray, her dog, had scarce set his eyes on the strange monster which came through the gate, than he set up such a barking, one would have thought all the rogues and robbers in the world were in the yard.

"Ah, deary me," said she, "I thought so; it can't be me surely." So she went to the strawyard, and the calves wouldn't lick her, when they snuffed the strong smell of tar.

"No, no!" she said, "it can't be me; it must be some strange, outlandish bird."

So she crept up on the roof of the storehouse and began to flap her arms, as if they had been wings, and was just going to fly off.

When her husband saw all this, out he came with his rifle, and began to take aim at her.

"Oh!" cried she, "don't shoot, don't shoot! It's only me."

"If it's you," said her husband, "don't stand up there like a goat on a housetop, but come down and let me hear what you have to say for yourself."

So she crawled down again, but she hadn't a shilling to show, for the shillings she had got from the butcher she had thrown away in her drunkenness. When her husband heard her story, he said, "You're only twice as silly as you were before," and he got so angry that he made up his mind to go away from her altogether, and never to come back till he had found three other women as silly as his own.

So he toddled off, and when he had walked a little way he saw a woman, who was running in and out of a newly-built wooden cottage with an empty sieve, and every time she ran in, she threw her apron over the sieve just as if she had something in it, and when she got in she turned it upside down on the floor.

"Why, mother," he asked, "what are you doing?"

"Oh," she answered, "I'm only carrying in a little sun; but I don't know how it is, when I'm outside, I have the sun in my sieve, but when I get inside, somehow or other I've thrown it away. But in my old cottage I had plenty of sun, though I never carried in the least bit. I only wish I knew someone who would bring the sun inside; I'd give him three hundred dollars and welcome."

"Have you got an axe?" asked the man. "If you have, I'll soon bring the sun inside."

So he got an axe and cut windows in the cottage, for the carpenters had forgotten them. Then the sun shone in, and he got his three hundred dollars.

"That was one of them," said the man to himself, as he went on his way.

After a while he passed by a house, out of which came an awful screaming and bellowing, so he turned in and saw a woman, who was hard at work banging her husband across the head with a beetle, and over his head she had drawn a shirt without any slit for the neck.

"Why, Mother!" he asked, "will you beat your husband to death?"

"No," she said, "I only must have a hole in this shirt for his neck to come through."

All the while the husband kept on screaming and calling out,

"Heaven help and comfort all who try on new shirts. If anyone would teach my wife another way of making a slit for the neck in my new shirts, I'd give him three hundred dollars down and welcome."

"I'll do it in the twinkling of an eye," said the man, "if you'll only give me a pair of scissors."

So he got a pair of scissors, and snipped a hole in the neck, and went off with his three hundred dollars.

"That was another of them," he said to himself, as he walked along.

Last of all, he came to a farm, where he made up his mind to rest a bit. So when he went in, the mistress asked him,

"Whence do you come, master?"

"Oh!" said he, "I come from Paradise Place," for that was the name of his farm.

"From Paradise Place!" she cried, "you don't say so! Why then you must know my second husband, Per, who is dead and gone, God rest his soul."

For you must know this woman had been married three times, and as her first and last husbands had been bad, she had made up her mind that the second only was gone to heaven.

"Oh, yes," said the man; "I know him very well."

"Well," asked the woman, "how do things go with him, poor dear soul?"

"Only middling," was the answer; "he goes about begging from house to house, and has neither food nor a rag to his back. As for money, he hasn't a sixpence to bless himself with."

"Mercy on me," cried out the woman; "he never ought to go about such a figure when he left so much behind him. Why, there's a whole cupboard full of old clothes upstairs which belonged to him, besides a great chest full of money yonder. Now, if you will take them with you, you shall have a horse and cart to carry them. As for the horse, he can keep it, and sit on the cart, and drive about from house to house, and then he needn't trudge on foot."

So the man got a whole cartload of clothes, and a chest full of shining dollars, and as much meat and drink as he would; and when he had got all he wanted, he jumped into the cart and drove off.

"That was the third," he said to himself, as he went along.

Now this woman's third husband was a little way off in a field ploughing, and when he saw a strange man driving off from the farm with his horse and cart, he went home and asked his wife who that was that had just started with the black horse.

"Oh, do you mean him?" said the wife. "Why, that was a man from Paradise, who said that Per, my dear second husband, who is dead and gone, is in a sad plight, and that he goes from house to house begging, and has neither clothes nor money; so I just sent him all those old clothes he left behind him, and the old money box with the dollars in it."

The man saw how the land lay in a trice, so he saddled his horse, and rode off from the farm at full gallop. It wasn't long before he was close behind the man who sat and drove the cart; but when the latter saw this he drove the cart into a thicket by the side of the road, pulled out a handful of hair from the horse's tail, jumped up on a little rise in the wood, where he tied the hair fast to a birch, and then lay down under it, and began to peer and stare up at the sky.

"Well, well, if I ever!" he said, as Per the third came riding up. "No! I never saw the like of this in all my born days!"

Then Per stood and looked at him for some time, wondering what had come over him; but at last he asked,

"What do you lie there staring at?"

"No," kept on the man, "I never did see anything like it!—here is a man going straight up to heaven on a black horse, and there you see his horse's tail still hanging in this birch; and yonder up in the sky you see the black horse."

Per looked first at the man, and then at the sky, and said,

"I see nothing but the horse hair in the birch; that's all I see!"

"Of course you can't, where you stand," said the man; "but just come and lie down here, and stare straight up, and mind you don't take your eyes off the sky; and then you shall see what you shall see."

But while Per the third lay and stared up at the sky till his eyes filled with tears, the man from Paradise Place took his horse and jumped on its back, and rode off both with it, and the cart and horse.

When the hoofs thundered along the road, Per the third jumped up; but he was so taken aback when he found the man had gone off with his horse that he hadn't the sense to run after him till it was too late.

He was rather down in the mouth when he got home to his wife; but when she asked him what he had done with the horse, he said,

"I gave it to the man, too, for Per the second, for I thought it wasn't right he should sit in a cart, and scramble about from house to house. So now he can sell the cart and buy himself a coach to drive about in."

"Thank you heartily!" said his wife; "I never thought you could be so kind."

Well, when the man reached home—who had got the six hundred dollars and the cartload of clothes and money—he saw that all his fields were ploughed and sown, and the first thing he asked his wife was, where she had got the seed-corn from.

"Oh," she said, "I have always heard that what a man sows he shall reap, so I sowed the salt which our friends the northcountry men laid up here with us, and if we only have rain I fancy it will come up nicely."

"Silly you are," said her husband, "and silly you will be so long as you live; but that is all one now, for the rest are not a bit wiser than you. There is not a pin to choose between you."

THE SQUIRE'S BRIDE

* * *

ONCE upon a time there was a wealthy squire who owned a large manor. He had silver in his chests and money that he loaned out at interest, but he lacked one thing, because he was a widower. One day the daughter of a neighboring farmer came to work on the manor. The squire liked her very much, and since she was the child of poor people, he thought he had only to hint at marriage, and she would agree on the spot. So he told her that it had occurred to him that maybe he had better marry again.

"Oh, well, so many things may occur to a person," said the girl, smiling a little; she thought that ugly old body might have thought of something more suitable than marriage.

"Now, the idea is, *you* were to become my wife," said the squire.

"Nay, thank you all the same, but that would never do," said the girl.

The squire was not used to taking no for an answer, and the less she wanted him, the more eager he was to get her. But since he could not make the girl listen to his proposals, he sent for her father and told him, that if he could arrange the marriage with his daughter, he would cancel the debt the other owed him, and into the bargain, he could have the bit of bottom land that lay beside his meadow.

Oh, to be sure, the father felt certain he would make his daughter see reason. She was a mere child and did not understand what was to her advantage, he said.

But for all his talk with his daughter, kindly or angrily, it did not help a bit. She would not marry the squire, not if he were sitting in ground gold to above his ears, she declared.

The squire waited many a day, but then he became angry and impatient. In the end he told the father of the girl, that if he expected him to stand by his offer, he had to bring the matter to an end, for he was tired of waiting.

The man said, he thought the best plan would be for the squire to get everything ready for the wedding, and when the minister and the wedding guests were assembled, he was to send for the girl, pretending that she was to do some work on the manor, and when she arrived he must wed her in a hurry, before she had had time to think of a way to escape.

This seemed to the squire a very sensible and good idea, and so they brewed and baked and prepared the house for the wedding, in great style.

When the wedding guests had arrived, the squire called one of his hired boys and told him to run over to the neighbor's on the south lot and tell him to send the thing he had promised.

"But unless you are back again in a jiffy, I'll..." he said and lifted his fist threateningly. He did not need to say more, for the boy was off, as if he had been burnt.

"Master says, his regards to you, and would you send him what you promised him, at once, because he is awfully busy today," said the boy to the man on the neighboring farm.

"Sure, just hurry down into my meadow, and take her with you, you'll find her there," said the neighbor.

The boy was off. When he came to the meadow, the daughter was there, raking hay. "I am here to fetch what your father promised master," he said.

Oh, you think you could fool me that easy! the girl thought. "Now is that so?" she said. "That would be our little yellow mare, I guess. You had better take her with you then; you will find her tethered on the other side of the pease field," the girl said.

The boy jumped on the back of the little yellow mare and rode home at a gallop.

"Did you bring her with you?" the squire said.

"She is outside by the front door," said the boy.

"Then take her upstairs to the room that was my late wife's," said the squire.

"Gracious me, how could I manage that?" said the boy.

"You do as I tell you," said the squire. "If you cannot manage her single-handed, call in some men to help you." He imagined the girl might make difficulties.

When the boy looked into the face of the squire he felt sure it was no use to reason with him. He went down and took with him all the farm hands. Some pulled in front, and some pushed from behind, and at long last they managed to get the mare upstairs and into the mistress' room. There the bridal finery was laid out.

"Well, I *did* it, master," the boy said. "But she was a tough job, the worst I ever set hands to on this manor."

"Ay, ay, I did not mean you were to do it for nothing," the master said. "Now tell the women to go up and dress her."

"Gracious me, I've never heard..." the boy said.

"Shut up and do as I tell you. They are to dress her, and don't let them forget either the garland or the crown," said the master.

The boy burst into the kitchen.

"Girls," he said, "listen—you are to go upstairs and dress the little yellow mare as a bride. Master must have planned to give his guests a big laugh."

Well, the girls decked out the little mare with all the finery there was, and the boy went down and announced that she was ready, garland and bridal crown and everything.

"That's good; bring her down then," said the master. "I'll receive her myself in the door of the drawing room."

There was an awful racket when she came downstairs, because she did not step lightly in satin slippers—not this bride! But when the door was thrown open, and the squire's bride entered the big drawing room, it cannot be denied, there was some tittering and chuckling among the guests. And the squire was so well satisfied with this bride, so people say, he never went a-wooing another.

THE MASTER THIEF

* ** ** *

ONCE upon a time there was a poor cottager who had three sons. He had nothing to leave them when he died, and no money with which to put them to any trade, so that he did not know what to make of them. At last he said he would give them leave to take to anything each liked best, and to go whithersoever they pleased, and he would go with them a bit of the way; and so he did. He went with them till they came to a place where three roads met, and there each of them chose a road, and their father bade them good-bye, and went back home. I have never heard tell what became of the two elder; but as for the youngest, he went both far and long, as you shall hear.

So it fell out one night as he was going through a great wood that bad weather overtook him. It blew, and sleeted, and drove so that he could scarce keep his eyes open; and in a trice, before he knew how it was, he got bewildered and could not find either road or path. But as he went on and on, at last he saw a glimmering of light far, far off in the wood. So he thought he would try and get to the light; and after a time he did reach it. There it was in a large house, and the fire was blazing so brightly inside, that he could tell the folk had not yet gone to bed; so he went in and saw an old dame bustling about and minding the house.

"Good evening!" said the youth.

"Good evening!" said the old dame.

"Hutetu! it's such foul weather out of doors tonight," said he.

"So it is," said she.

"Can I get leave to have a bed and shelter here tonight?" asked the youth.

"You'll get no good by sleeping here," said the old dame; "for if the folk come home and find you here, they'll kill both me and you."

"What sort of folk, then, are they who live here?" asked the youth.

"Oh, robbers! and a bad lot of them too," said the old dame. "They stole me away when I was little, and have kept me as their housekeeper ever since."

"Well, for all that, I think I'll just go to bed," said the youth. "Come what may, I'll not stir out at night in such weather."

"Very well," said the old dame; "but if you stay, it will be the worse for you."

With that the youth got into a bed which stood there, but he dared not go to sleep, and very soon after in came the robbers; so the old dame told them how a stranger fellow had come in whom she had not been able to get out of the house again.

"Did you see if he had any money?" said the robbers.

"Such a one as he money!" said the old dame; "the tramper! Why, if he had clothes to his back, it was as much as he had."

Then the robbers began to talk among themselves what they should do with him; if they should kill him outright, or what else they should do. Meantime the youth got up and began to talk to them, and to ask if they didn't want a servant, for it might be that he would be glad to enter their service.

"Oh," said they, "if you have a mind to follow the trade that we follow, you can very well get a place here."

"It's all one to me what trade I follow," said the youth; "for when I left home, father gave me leave to take to any trade I chose."

"Well, have you a mind to steal?" asked the robbers.

"I don't care," said the youth, for he thought it would not take long to learn that trade.

Now there lived a man a little way off who had three oxen. One of these he was to take to the town to sell, and the robbers had heard what he was going to do, so they said to the youth, if he were good to steal the ox from the man by the way without his knowing it, and without doing him any harm, they would give him leave to be their serving-man.

Well! the youth set off, and took with him a pretty shoe, with a silver buckle on it, which lay about the house; and he put the shoe in the road along which the man was going with his ox; and when he had done that, he went into the wood and hid himself under a bush. So when the man came by he saw the shoe at once.

"That's a nice shoe," said he. "If I only had the fellow to it, I'd take it home with me, and perhaps I'd put my old dame in a good humour for once." For you must know he had an old wife, so cross and snappish, it was not long between each time that she boxed his ears. But when he bethought him that he could do nothing with the odd shoe unless he had the fellow to it; so he went on his way and let the shoe lie on the road.

Then the youth took up the shoe, and made all the haste he could to get before the man by a shortcut through the wood, and laid it down before him in the road again. When the man came along with his ox, he got quite angry with himself for being so dull as to leave the fellow to the shoe lying in the road instead of taking it with him; so he tied the ox to the fence, and said to himself, "I may just as well run back and pick up the other, and then I'll have a pair of good shoes for my old dame, and so, perhaps, I'll get a kind word from her for once."

So he set off, and hunted and hunted up and down for the shoe, but no shoe did he find; and at length he had to go back with the one he had. But, meanwhile, the youth had taken the ox and gone off with it; and when the man came and saw his ox gone, he began to cry and bewail, for he was afraid his old dame would kill him outright when she came to know that the ox was lost. But just then it came across his mind that he would go home and take the second ox, and drive it to the town, and not let his old dame know anything about the matter. So he did this, and went home and took the ox without his dame's knowing it, and set off with it to the town. But the robbers knew all about it, and they said to the youth, if he could get this ox too without the man's knowing it, and without his doing him any harm, he should be as good as any one of them. If that were all, the youth said, he did not think it a very hard thing.

This time he took with him a rope and hung himself up under the arm-pits to a tree right in the man's way. So the man came along with his ox, and when he saw such a sight hanging there he began to feel a little queer.

"Well," said he, "whatever heavy thoughts you had who have hanged yourself up there, it can't be helped; you may hang for what I care! I can't breathe life into you again"; and with that he went on his way with his ox. Down slipped the youth from the tree, and ran by a footpath, and got before the man, and hung himself up right in his way again.

"Bless me!" said the man, "were you really so heavy at heart that you hanged yourself up there—or is it only a piece of witchcraft that I see before me? Aye, aye! you may hang for all I care, whether you are a ghost or whatever you are." So he passed on with his ox.

Now the youth did just as he had done twice before; he jumped down from the tree, ran through the wood by a footpath, and hung himself up right in the man's way again. But when the man saw this sight for the third time, he said to himself—

"Well! this is an ugly business! Is it likely now that they should have been so heavy at heart as to hang themselves, all these three? No! I cannot think it is anything else than a piece of witchcraft that I see. But now I'll soon know for certain; if the other two are still hanging there, it must be really so; but if they are not, then it can be nothing but witchcraft that I see."

So he tied his ox, and ran back to see if the others were still really hanging there. But while he went and peered up into all the trees, the youth jumped down and took his ox and ran off with it. When the man came back and found his ox gone he was in a sad plight, and, as anyone might know without being told, he began to cry and bemoan; but at last he came to take it easier, and so he thought,

"There's no other help for it than to go home and take the third ox without my dame's knowing it, and to try and drive a good bargain with it, so that I may get a good sum of money."

So he went home and set off with the ox, and his old dame new never a word about the matter. But the robbers, they new all about it, and they said to the youth, that if he could steal this ox as he had stolen the other two, then he should be master over the whole band. Well, the youth set off, and ran into the wood; and as the man came by with his ox he set up a dreadful bellowing, just like a great ox in the wood. When the man heard that, you can't think how glad he was, for it seemed to him that he knew the voice of his big bullock, and he thought that now he should find both of them again; so he tied up the third ox, and ran off from the road to look for them in the wood; but in the meantime the youth went off with the third ox. Now, when the man came back and found he had lost this ox too, he was so wild that there was no end to his grief. He cried and roared and beat his breast, and, to tell the truth, it was many days before he dared go home; for he was afraid lest his old dame should kill him outright on the spot.

As for the robbers, they were not very well pleased either, when they had to own that the youth was master over the whole band. So one day they thought they would try their hands at something which he was not man enough to do; and they set off all together, every man Jack of them, and left him alone at home. Now, the first thing that he did when they were all well clear of the house, was to drive the oxen out to the road, so that they might run back to the man from whom he had stolen them; and right glad he was to see them, as you may fancy. Next he took all the horses which the robbers had, and loaded them with the best things he could lay his hands on—gold and silver, and clothes and other fine things; and then he bade the old dame to greet the robbers when they came back, and to thank them for him, and to say that now he was setting off on his travels, and they would have hard work to find him again; and with that, off he started.

After a good bit he came to the road along which he was going when he fell among the robbers, and when he got near home, and could see his father's cottage, he put on a uniform which he had found among the clothes he had taken from the robbers, and which was made just like a general's. So he drove up to the door as if he were any other great man. After that he went in and asked if he could have a lodging? No; that he couldn't at any price.

"How ever should I be able," said the man, "to make room in my house for such a fine gentleman—I who scarce have a rag to lie upon, and miserable rags too?"

"You always were a stingy old hunk," said the youth, "and so you are still, when you won't take your own son in."

"What, you my son!" said the man.

"Don't you know me again?" said the youth. Well, after a little while he did know him again.

"But what have you been turning your hand to, that you have made yourself so great a man in such haste?" asked the man.

"Oh! I'll soon tell you," said the youth. "You said I might take to any trade I chose, and so I bound myself apprentice to a pack of thieves and robbers, and now I've served my time out, and am become a Master Thief."

Now there lived a Squire close by to his father's cottage, and he had such a great house, and such heaps of money, he could not tell how much he had. He had a daughter too, and a smart and pretty girl she was. So the Master Thief set his heart upon having her to wife, and he told his father to go to the Squire and ask for his daughter for him.

"If he asks by what trade I get my living, you can say I'm a Master Thief."

"I think you've lost your wits," said the man, "for you can't be in your right mind when you think of such stuff."

No! he had not lost his wits, his father must and should go to the Squire and ask for his daughter.

"Nay, but I tell you, I daren't go to the Squire and be your spokesman; he who is so rich, and has so much money," said the man.

Yes, there was no help for it, said the Master Thief; he should go whether he would or no; and if he did not go by fair means, he would soon make him go by foul. But the man was still loath to go; so he stepped after him, and rubbed him down with a good birch cudgel, and kept on till the man came crying and sobbing inside the Squire's door.

"How now, my man! what ails you?" said the Squire.

So he told him the whole story; how he had three sons who set off one day, and how he had given them leave to go whithersoever they would, and to follow whatever calling they chose. "And here now is the youngest come home, and has thrashed me till he has made me come to you and ask for your daughter for him to wife; and he bids me say, besides, that he's a Master Thief." And so he fell to crying and sobbing again.

"Never mind, my man," said the Squire laughing; "just go back and tell him from me, he must prove his skill first. If he can steal the roast from the spit in the kitchen on Sunday, while all the household are looking after it, he shall have my daughter. Just go and tell him that."

So he went back and told the youth, who thought it would be an easy job. So he set about and caught three hares alive, and put them into a bag, and dressed himself in some old rags, until he looked so poor and filthy that it made one's heart bleed to see; and then he stole into the passage at the back-door of the Squire's house on the Sunday forenoon, with his bag, just like any other beggar-boy. But the Squire himself and all his household were in the kitchen watching the roast. Just as they were doing this, the youth let one hare go, and it set off and ran round and round the yard in front of the house.

"Oh, just look at that hare!" said the folk in the kitchen, and were all for running out to catch it.

Yes, the Squire saw it running too. "Oh, let it run," said he; "there's no use in thinking to catch a hare on the spring."

A little while after, the youth let the second hare go, and they saw it in the kitchen, and thought it was the same they had seen before, and still wanted to run out and catch it; but the Squire said again it was no use. It was not long before the youth let the third hare go, and it set off and ran round and round the yard as the others before it. Now, they saw it from the kitchen, and still thought it was the same hare that kept on running about, and were all eager to be out after it.

"Well, it is a fine hare," said the Squire; "come, let's see if we can't lay our hands on it."

So out he ran, and the rest with him—away they all went, the hare before, and they after; so that it was rare fun to see. But meantime the youth took the roast and ran off with it; and where the Squire got a roast for his dinner that day I don't know; but one thing I know, and that is, that he had no roast hare, though he ran after it till he was both warm and weary.

Now it chanced that the Parson came to dinner that day, and when the Squire told him what a trick the Master Thief had played him, he made such game of him that there was no end of it.

"For my part," said the Parson, "I can't think how it could ever happen to me to be made such a fool of by a fellow like that."

"Very well—only keep a sharp look-out," said the Squire; "maybe he'll come to see you before you know a word of it. But the Parson stuck to his text—that he did, and made game of the Squire because he had been so taken in.

Later in the afternoon came the Master Thief, and wanted to have the Squire's daughter, as he had given his word. But the Squire began to talk him over, and said, "Oh, you must first prove your skill a little more; for what you did today was no great thing, after all. Couldn't you now play off a good trick on the Parson, who is sitting in there, and making game of me for letting such a fellow as you twist me round his thumb."

"Well, as for that, it wouldn't be hard," said the Master Thief. So he dressed himself up like an angel, threw a great white sheet over his body, took the wings of a goose and tied them to his back, and so climbed up into a great maple which stood in the Parson's garden. And when the Parson came home in the evening, the youth began to bawl out—

"Mr. Laurence! Mr. Laurence!"—for that was the Parson's name.

"Who is that calling me?" said the Parson.

"I am an angel," said the Master Thief, "sent from God to let you know that you shall be taken up alive into heaven for your piety's sake. Next Monday night you must hold yourself ready for the journey, for I shall come then to fetch you in a sack; and all your gold and your silver, and all that you have of this world's goods, you must lay together in a heap in your dining-room."

Well, Mr. Laurence fell on his knees before the angel, and thanked him; and the very next day he preached a farewell sermon, and gave it out how there had come down an angel unto the big maple in his garden, who had told him that he was to be taken up alive into heaven for his piety's sake; and he preached and made such a touching discourse, that all who were at church wept, both young and old.

So the next Monday night came the Master Thief like an angel again, and the Parson fell on his knees and thanked him before he was put into the sack; but when he had got him well in, the Master Thief drew and dragged him over stocks and stones.

"Ow! Ow!" groaned the Parson inside the sack. "Wherever are we going?"

"This is the narrow way which leadeth into the kingdom of heaven," said the Master Thief, who went on dragging him along till he had nearly broken every bone in his body. At last he tumbled him into a goose-house that belonged to the Squire, and the geese began pecking and picking him with their bills, so that he was more dead than alive.

"Now you are in the flames of purgatory, to be cleansed and purified for life everlasting," said the Master Thief; and with that he went his way, and took all the gold which the Parson had laid together in his dining-room. The next morning, when the goose-girl came to let the geese out, she heard how the Parson lay in the sack and bemoaned himself in the goose-house.

"In heaven's name, who's there, and what ails you?" she cried.

"Oh!" said the Parson, "if you are an angel from heaven, do let me out, and let me return again to earth, for it is worse here than in hell. The little fiends keep on pinching me with tongs."

"God help us, I am no angel at all," said the girl, as she helped the Parson out of the sack; "I only look after the Squire's geese, and like enough they are the little fiends which have pinched your Reverence."

"Oh!" groaned the Parson, "this is all that Master Thief's doing. Ah! my gold and my silver, and my fine clothes!" And he beat his breast, and hobbled home at such a rate that the girl thought he had lost his wits all at once.

Now when the Squire came to hear how it had gone with the Parson, and how he had been along the narrow way, and into purgatory, he laughed till he well-nigh split his sides. But when the Master Thief came and asked for his daughter as he had promised, the Squire put him off again, and said—

"You must do one masterpiece better still, that I may see plainly what you are fit for. Now, I have twelve horses in my stable, and on them I will put twelve grooms—one on each. If you are so good a thief as to steal the horses from under them, I'll see what I can do for you."

"Very well, I daresay I can do it," said the Master Thief; "but shall I really have your daughter if I can?"

"Yes, if you can, I'll do my best for you," said the Squire.

So the Master Thief set off to a shop, and bought brandy enough to fill two pocket-flasks, and into one of them he put a sleepy drink, but into the other only brandy. After that he hired eleven men to lie in wait at night, behind the Squire's stableyard; and last of all, for fair words and a good bit of money, he borrowed a ragged gown and cloak from an old woman; and so, with a staff in his hand, and a bundle at his back, he limped off, as evening drew on, towards the

Squire's stable. Just as he got there they were watering the horses for the night, and had their hands full of work.

"What the devil do you want?" said one of the grooms to the old woman.

"Oh, oh! hutetu! it is so bitter cold," said she, and shivered and shook, and made wry faces. "Hutetu! it is so cold, a poor wretch may easily freeze to death"; and with that she fell to shivering and shaking again.

"Oh! for the love of heaven, can I get leave to stay here a while, and sit inside the stable door?"

"To the devil with your leave," said one. "Pack yourself off this minute, for if the Squire sets his eyes on you, he'll lead us a pretty dance."

"Oh! the poor old bag-of-bones," said another, whose heart took pity on her, "the old hag may sit inside and welcome; such a one as she can do no harm."

And the rest said, some she should stay, and some she shouldn't; but while they were quarreling and minding the horses, she crept further and further into the stable, till at last she sat herself down behind the door; and when she had got so far, no one gave any more heed to her.

As the night wore on, the men found it rather cold work to sit so still and quiet on horseback.

"Hutetu! it is so devilish cold," said one, and beat his arms crosswise.

"That it is," said another; "I freeze so, that my teeth chatter."

"If one only had a quid to chew," said a third. Well! there was one who had an ounce or two; so they shared it between them, though it wasn't much, after all, that each got; and so they chewed and spat, and spat and chewed. This helped them somewhat; but in a little while they were just as bad as ever.

"Hutetu!" said one, and shivered and shook.

"Hutetu!" said the old woman, and shivered so, that every tooth in her head chattered. Then she pulled out the flask with brandy in it, and her hand shook so that the spirit splashed about in the flask, and then she took such a gulp, that it went "bop" in her throat.

"What's that you've got in your flask, old girl?" said one of the grooms.

"Oh! it's only a drop of brandy, old man," said she.

"Brandy! Well, I never! Do let me have a drop," screamed the whole twelve, one after another.

"Oh! but it is such a little drop," mumbled the old woman, "it will not even wet your mouths round." But they must and would have it; there was no help for it; and so she pulled out the flask with the sleepy drink in it, and put it to the first man's lips; then she shook no more, but guided the flask so that each of them got what he wanted, and the twelfth had not done drinking before the first sat and snored. Then the Master Thief threw off his beggar's rags, and took one groom after the other so softly off their horses, and set them astride on the beams between the stalls; and so he called his eleven men, and rode off with the Squire's twelve horses.

But when the Squire got up in the morning, and went to look after his grooms, they had just begun to come to; and some of them fell to spurring the beams with their spurs, till the splinters flew again, and some fell off, and some still hung on and sat there looking like fools.

"Ho! ho!" said the Squire; "I see very well who has been here; but as for you, a pretty set of blockheads you must be to sit here and let the Master Thief steal the horses from between your legs."

So they all got a good leathering because they had not kept a sharper look-out.

Further on in the day came the Master Thief again, and told

how he had managed the matter, and asked for the Squire's daughter, as he had promised; but the Squire gave him one hundred dollars down, and said he must do something better still.

"Do you think now," said he, "you can steal the horse from under me while I am out riding on his back?"

"Oh, yes! I daresay I could," said the Master Thief, "if I were really sure of getting your daughter."

Well, well, the Squire would see what he could do; and he told the Master Thief a day when he would be taking a ride on a great common where they drilled the troops. So the Master Thief soon got hold of an old worn-out jade of a mare, and set to work, and made traces and collar of withies and broom-twigs, and bought an old beggarly cart and a great cask. After that he told an old beggar woman, he would give her ten dollars if she would get inside the cask, and keep her mouth agape over the taphole, into which he was going to stick his finger. No harm should happen to her; she should only be driven about a little; and if he took his finger out more than once, she was to have ten dollars more. Then he threw a few rags and tatters over himself, and stuffed himself out, and put on a wig and a great beard of goat's hair, so that no one could know him, and set off for the common where the Squire had already been riding about a good bit. When he reached the place, he went along so softly and slowly that he scarce made an inch of way. "Gee up! Gee up," and so he went on a little; then he stood stock still, and so on a little again; and altogether the pace was so poor it never once came into the Squire's head that this could be the Master Thief.

At last the Squire rode right up to him, and asked if he had seen anyone lurking about in the wood thereabouts.

"No," said the man, "I haven't seen a soul."

"Hark ye, now," said the Squire, "if you have a mind to ride into the wood, and hunt about and see if you can fall upon anyone lurking about there, you shall have the loan of my horse, and a shilling into the bargain, to drink my health, for your pains."

"I don't see how I can go," said the man, "for I am going to a wedding with this cask of mead, which I have been to town to fetch, and here the tap has fallen out by the way, and so I must go along, holding my finger in the taphole."

"Ride off," said the Squire; "I'll look after your horse and cask."

Well, on these terms the man was willing to go; but he begged the Squire to be quick in putting his finger into the taphole when he took his own out, and to mind and keep it there till he came back. At last the Squire grew weary of standing there with his finger in the taphole, so he took it out.

"Now I shall have ten dollars more," screamed the old woman inside the cask; and then the Squire saw at once how the land lay, and took himself off home; but he had not gone far before they met him with a fresh horse, for the Master Thief had already been to his house, and told them to send one.

The day after, he came to the Squire and would have his daughter, as he had given his word; but the Squire put him off again with fine words, and gave him two hundred dollars, and said he must do one more masterpiece. If he could do that, he should have her. Well, well, the Master Thief thought he could do it, if he only knew what it was to be.

"Do you think, now," said the Squire; "you can steal the sheet off our bed, and the shift off my wife's back? Do you think you could do that?"

"It shall be done," said the Master Thief. "I only wish I was as sure of getting your daughter."

So when night began to fall, the Master Thief went out and cut down a thief who hung on the gallows, and threw him across his shoulders, and carried him off. Then he got a long ladder and set it up against the Squire's bedroom window, and so climbed up, and kept bobbing the dead man up and down, just for all the world like one that was peeping in at the window.

"That's the Master Thief, old lass!" said the Squire, and gave his wife a nudge on the side. "Now see if I don't shoot him, that's all."

So saying he took up a rifle which he had laid at his bedside.

"No! no! pray don't shoot him after telling him he might come and try," said his wife.

"Don't talk to me, for shoot him I will," said he; and so he lay there and aimed and aimed; but as soon as the head came up before the window, and he saw a little of it, so soon was it down again. At last he thought he had a good aim; "bang" went the gun, down fell the dead body to the ground with a heavy thump, and down the Master Thief as fast as he could.

"Well," said the Squire, "it is quite true that I am the chief magistrate in these parts; but people are fond of talking, and it would be a bore if they came to see this dead man's body. I think the best thing to be done is that I should go down and bury him."

"You must do as you think best, dear," said his wife. So the Squire got out of bed and went downstairs, and he had scarce put his foot out of the door before the Master Thief stole in, and went straight upstairs to the Squire's wife.

"Why, dear, back already?" said she, for she thought it was her husband.

"Oh, yes, I only just put him into a hole, and threw a little earth over him. It is enough that he is out of sight, for it's such a bad night out of doors; by-and-by I'll do it better. But just let me have the sheet to wipe myself with—he was so bloody—and I have made myself in such a mess with him."

So he got the sheet.

After a while he said—

"Do you know I am afraid you must let me have your night-shift too, for the sheet won't do by itself; that I can see."

So she gave him the shift also. But just then it came across his mind that he had forgotten to lock the house-door, so he must step down and lock that before he came back to bed, and away he went with both shift and sheet.

A little while after came the Squire.

"Why! what a time you've taken to lock the door, dear!" said his wife; "and what have you done with the sheet and shift that you had to wipe off the blood," said she.

"What the Hell!" said the Squire; "has he taken me in this time too?"

Next day came the Master Thief and asked for the Squire's daughter, as he had given his word; and then the Squire dared not do anything else than give her to him, and a good lump of money into the bargain; for to tell the truth, he was afraid lest the Master Thief should steal the eyes out of his head, and that the people would begin to say spiteful things of him if he broke his word. So the Master Thief lived well and happily from that time forward. I don't know whether he stole any more; but if he did, I am quite sure it was only for the sake of a bit of fun.

THE PARSON
AND THE SEXTON

* * *

ONCE upon a time there was a Parson, who thought he was such a big shot, he roared from afar, when he saw somebody driving towards him on the highroad: "Give way, give way, here comes the Parson in person."

One day when he travelled along and made a nuisance of himself, he met the King. "Give way, give way," he roared from afar. But the King drove on, and this time it was the Parson who had to give way and turn his horse out into the road-side. But when the King came up alongside the Parson he said: "Meet me tomorrow at my manor, and unless you can answer the three questions I am going to ask you, you'll lose both gown and ruff, because of your arrogance."

This was different from what the Parson was used to. Holler and roar and behave like the worst bully he could as well as anybody, but questions and answers were not his line. So he called on the Sexton, of whom people said, he would have fitted better into the gown than did the Parson. He told the Sexton he did not want to go, "Because a fool may ask more than ten wise men can answer," he said, and so he persuaded the Sexton to go instead of him.

Well, the Sexton set out and came to the King's manor, dressed in the Parson's gown and ruff. The King received him on the porch, and he had on his crown and scepter, radiant in all his splendor.

"Oh, so there you are!" said the King.

To be sure, yes here he was.

"Now tell me first," said the King. "How far is it from the East to the West?"

"One day's voyage," said the Sexton.

"How so?" asked the King.

"Well, you see, the sun rises in the East and sets in the West, and she easily travels that distance in a day," said the Sexton.

"Well, well," said the King. "But now tell me," he said, "how much would you say I am worth, such as you see me here?"

"Now since Christ was estimated to be worth thirty silver dollars, I suppose I dare not set your value higher than twenty-nine," said the Sexton.

"Haw, haw," said the King. "Now, since you are so wise about many things, tell me what I am thinking this moment?"

"Oh, you think it is the Parson you have before you now, but with your leave, you are mistaken, for *it is* the Sexton," he said.

"Well then, go home, you—and tell the Parson that you are to be the Parson, and he is to be the Sexton," said the King. And so it had to be.

EAST O' THE SUN
AND WEST O' THE MOON

* * *

ONCE on a time there was a poor husbandman who had so many children that he hadn't much of either food or clothing to give them. Pretty children they all were, but the prettiest was the youngest daughter, who was so lovely there was no end to her loveliness.

So one day, 'twas on a Thursday evening late in the fall of the year, the weather was wild and rough outside, and it was cruelly dark, and the rain fell and the wind blew, till the walls of the cottage shook again. There they all sat round the fire busy with this and that. Just then, all at once, something gave three taps on the windowpane. The father went out to see what was the matter; and, when he got out of doors, what should he see but a great big White Bear!

"Good evening to you!" said the White Bear.

"The same to you," said the man.

"Will you give me your youngest daughter? If you will, I'll make you as rich as you are now poor," said the Bear.

Well, the man would not be at all sorry to be so rich; but still he thought he must have a bit of a talk with his daughter first. So he went in and told them how there was a great White Bear waiting outside, who had given his word to make them rich if he could only have the youngest daughter.

The girl said no, outright. Nothing could get her to say anything else; so the man went out and settled with the White Bear, that he should come again the next Thursday evening to get an answer. Meantime he talked to his daughter, and kept on telling her of all the riches they would get, and how well off she, herself, would be. And so at last she thought better of it, and washed and mended her rags, made herself as smart as she could, and was ready to start. It was not much she was bringing with her! The next Thursday evening when the White Bear came to fetch her, she got upon his back with her bundle, and off they went. When they had gone a bit of the way, the White Bear said,

"Are you afraid?"

"No!" she said.

"Well, mind you hold tight by my shaggy coat, and then there's nothing to fear," said the Bear.

So she rode a long, long way, till they came to a great steep hill. There, on the face of it, the White Bear gave a knock, and a door opened. They came into a castle, where there were many rooms all lit up—rooms gleaming with silver and gold. There, too, was a table ready laid; and it was all as grand as grand could be. Then the White Bear gave her a silver bell; when she wanted anything, she was only to ring it, and she would get it at once.

Well, after she had eaten and drunk, evening wore on, she got sleepy after her journey, and thought she would like to go to bed, so she rang the bell; and she had scarce taken hold of it before she came into a chamber, where there was a bed made, as fair and white as anyone would wish to sleep in, with silken pillows and curtains, and gold fringe. All that was in the room was gold or silver; but when she had gone to bed, and put out the light, a man came and laid himself alongside her. That was the White Bear, who threw off his beast shape at night. But she never saw him, for he always came after she had put out the light, and before the day dawned he was up and off again.

Things went on happily for a while, but at last she began to get silent and sorrowful; for she went about all day alone, and she longed to go home to see her father and mother, and brothers and sisters. So one day, when the White Bear asked what it was that she lacked, she said it was dull and lonely there, and that she longed to go home to see her father and mother, and brothers and sisters, and that she was sad and sorrowful because she couldn't get to them.

"Well, well!" said the Bear, "perhaps there's a cure for all this; but you must promise me one thing—not to talk alone with your mother, but only when the rest are by to hear; for she'll take you by the hand and try to lead you into a room alone to talk. But you must mind and not do that, else you'll make both of us miserable."

So one Sunday the White Bear came and said that now they could set off to see her father and mother. Well, off they started, she sitting on his back. They went far and long. At last they came to a grand house, and there her brothers and sisters were running about out of doors at play, and everything was so pretty, 'twas a joy to see.

"This is where your father and mother live now," said the White Bear; "but don't forget what I told you, else you'll make us both miserable."

No! bless her, she'd not forget, and when she had reached the house, the White Bear turned right about and left her.

Then when she went in to see her father and mother, there was such joy, there was no end to it. None of them could thank her enough for all she had done for them. Now, they had everything they wished, as good as good could be, and they all wanted to know how she got on where she lived.

"Well, she said, it was very good to live where she did; she had all she wished. What she said besides I don't know; but I don't think

any of them had the right end of the stick, or that they got much out
of her. But in the afternoon, after they had finished dinner, all happened as the White Bear had said. Her mother wanted to talk with
her alone in her bedroom; but she minded what the White Bear had
said, and wouldn't go upstairs.

"Oh! what we have to talk about will keep," she said and put
her mother off. But somehow or other, her mother got round her at
last, and she had to tell her the whole story. So she said, how every
night, when she had gone to bed, a man came and lay down beside
her as soon as she had put out the light, and how she never saw him,
because he was always up and away before the morning dawned;
and how she went about woeful and sorrowing, for she thought she
should so like to see him; and how all day long she walked about
there alone, and how dull and dreary and lonesome it was.

"My!" said her mother, "it may well be a troll you sleep with!
But now I'll teach you how to set eyes on him. I'll give you a bit
of candle which you can carry home in your bosom. Just light that
while he is asleep, but take care not to drop the tallow on him."

So she took the candle, and hid it in her bosom, and as night
drew on, the White Bear came and fetched her away.

But when they had gone a bit of the way, the White Bear asked
if all hadn't happened as he had said.

Well, she couldn't say it hadn't.

"Now, mind," said he, "if you have listened to your mother's
advice, you have brought bad luck on us both, and then, all that has
passed between us will be as nothing."

No, she said she hadn't listened to her mother's advice.

So when she reached home, and had gone to bed, it was the old
story over again. There came a man and lay down beside her. But at
dead of night, when she heard he slept, she got up and struck a light,
lit the candle, and let the light shine on him, and so she saw that he

was the loveliest Prince one could ever set eyes on, and she fell so deeply in love with him, on the spot, that she thought she couldn't live if she didn't give him a kiss there and then. And so she did, but as she kissed him, she dropped three hot drops of tallow on his shirt, and he woke up.

"What have you done?" he cried; "now you have made us both miserable, for had you held out only this one year, I had been freed; for I have a stepmother who has bewitched me, so that I am a White Bear by day, and a Man by night. But now all ties are snapped between us; I must set off from you to her. She lives in a castle that stands East O' the Sun and West O' the Moon, and there, too, is a Princess, with a nose three ells long, and she's the wife I must have now."

She wept and took it ill, but there was no help for it; go he must.

Then she asked if she mightn't go with him?

No, she mightn't.

"Tell me the way, then," she said, "and I'll search you out; that surely I may get leave to do."

Yes, she might do that, he said; but there was no way to that place. It lay East O' the Sun and West O' the Moon, and thither she'd never find her way.

So next morning, when she woke up, both Prince and castle were gone, and there she lay on a little green patch, in the midst of the gloomy thick wood, and by her side lay the same bundle of rags she had brought with her from her old home. So when she had rubbed the sleep out of her eyes, and wept till she was tired, she set out on her way, and walked many, many days, till she came to a lofty crag. Under it sat an old hag who played with a gold apple which she tossed about. The girl asked her if she knew the way to the Prince, who lived with his stepmother in the castle, that lay East O' the Sun and West O' the Moon, and who was to marry the Princess with a nose three ells long.

"How did you come to know about him?" asked the old hag. "But maybe you are the girl who ought to have had him?"

Yes, she was.

"So, so; it's you, is it?" said the old hag. "Well, all I know about him is, that he lives in the castle that lies East O' the Sun and West O' the Moon, and thither you'll come, late or never; but still you may have the loan of my horse, and on him you can ride to my next neighbor. Maybe she'll be able to tell you. And when you get there, just give the horse a switch under the left ear, and beg him to be off home. But stay, this gold apple you may take with you."

So she got upon the horse, and rode a long, long time, till she came to another crag, under which sat another old hag, with a gold carding comb. The girl asked her if she knew the way to the castle that lay East O' the Sun and West O' the Moon and she answered, like the first old hag, that she knew nothing about it, except it was East O' the Sun and West O' the Moon.

"And thither you'll come, late or never, but you shall have the loan of my horse to my next neighbor; maybe she'll tell you all about it. And when you get there, just switch the horse under the left ear, and beg him to be off home."

And this old hag gave her the golden carding comb; it might be she'd find some use for it, she said. So the girl got up on the horse, and rode a far, far way, and a weary time; and so at last she came to another great crag, under which sat another old hag, spinning with a golden spinning-wheel. Her, too, she asked if she knew the way to the Prince, and where the castle was that lay East O' the Sun and West O' the Moon. So it was the same thing over again.

"Maybe it's you who ought to have had the Prince?" said the old hag.

Yes, it was.

But she, too, didn't know the way a bit better than the other two. "East O' the Sun and West O' the Moon it was," she knew—that was all.

"And thither you'll come late or never; but I'll lend you my horse, and then I think you'd best ride to the East Wind and ask him; maybe he knows those parts, and can blow you thither. But when you get to him, you need only give the horse a switch under the left ear, and he'll trot home of himself."

And then she gave her a gold spinning-wheel. "Maybe you'll find a use for it," said the old hag.

Then on rode the girl for many, many days, a weary time, before she got to the East Wind's house, but at last she did reach it. She asked the East Wind if he could tell her the way to the Prince who dwelt East O' the Sun and West O' the Moon. Yes, the East Wind had often heard tell of it, and the Prince and the castle, but he couldn't tell the way, for he had never blown so far.

"But, if you will, I'll go with you to my brother the West Wind; maybe he knows, for he's much stronger. So, if you will just get on my back, I'll carry you thither." Yes, she got on his back, and I should just think they went briskly along.

When they got there, they went into the West Wind's house, and the East Wind said the girl he had brought was the one who ought to have had the Prince who lived in the castle East O' the Sun and West O' the Moon. And so she had set out to seek him, and he had come with her, and would be glad to know if the West Wind knew how to get to the castle.

"Nay," said the West Wind, "so far I've never blown; but if you will, I'll go with you to our brother the South Wind, for he's much stronger than either of us, and has flapped his wings far and wide. Maybe he'll tell you. You can get on my back, and I'll carry you to him."

So she got on his back, and thus they travelled to the South Wind, and I don't believe they were very long on the way.

When they got there, the West Wind asked him if he could tell the girl the way to the castle that lay East O' the Sun and West O' the Moon, for it was she who ought to have had the Prince who lived there.

"You don't say so! That's she, is it?" said the South Wind.

"Well, I have blustered about in most places in my time, but so far have I never blown; but if you will, I'll take you to my brother the North Wind. He is the oldest and strongest of the whole lot of us, and if he doesn't know where it is, you'll never find anyone in the world to tell you. You can get on my back, and I'll carry you thither."

And so she got on his back, and away he went from his house at a fine rate. And this time, too, she wasn't long on her way.

When they got to the North Wind's house, he was so wild and cross, they could feel cold puffs come from him while still a long way off.

"Blast you both; what do you want?" he roared out to them from ever so far off, so that it struck them with an icy shiver.

"Well," said the South Wind, "you needn't be so foul-mouthed, for here I am, your brother, the South Wind, and here is the girl who ought to have had the Prince who dwells in the castle that lies East O' the Sun and West O' the Moon, and now she wants to ask you if you ever were there, and can tell her the way, for she would be so glad to find him again."

"Yes, I know well enough where it is," said the North Wind. "Once in my life I blew an aspen leaf thither, but I was so tired I couldn't blow a puff for ever so many days. But if you really wish to go thither, and aren't afraid to come along with me, I'll take you on my back and see if I can blow you that far."

Yes! with all her heart; she must and would get thither if it were possible in any way; and as for fear, however madly he went, she wouldn't be at all afraid.

"Very well, then," said the North Wind, "but you must sleep here tonight, for we must have the whole day before us, if we're to get there at all."

Early next morning the North Wind woke her, and puffed himself up, and blew himself out, and made himself so stout and big, 'twas gruesome to look at him. And so, off they went, high up through the air, as if they would never stop till they got to the world's end.

Down below there was such a storm, it threw down long tracts of wood and many houses, and when it swept over the great sea, ships foundered by the hundreds.

So they tore on and on—no one can believe how far they went— and all the while they still went over the sea, and the North Wind got more and more weary, and so out of breath he could scarce bring out a puff, and his wings drooped and drooped, and drooped, till at last he sunk so low that the crests of the waves dashed over his heels.

"Are you afraid?" said the North Wind.

No, she wasn't.

But they weren't very far from land; and the North Wind had still so much strength left in him that he managed to throw her up on the shore under the windows of the castle that lay East O' the Sun and West O' the Moon. By then he was so weak and worn out, he had to stay there and rest many days before he could get home again.

Next morning the girl sat down under the castle window, and began to play with the gold apple; and the first person she saw was the Long-nose who was to have the Prince.

"What do you want for your gold apple, you lassie?" said the Long-nose, and threw up the window.

"It's not for sale, for gold or money," said the girl.

"If it's not for sale for gold or money, what is it that you will sell it for? You may name your own price," said the Princess.

"Well! if I may get to the Prince, who lives here, and be with him tonight, you shall have it," said the girl whom the North Wind had brought.

Yes she might; that could be done. So the Princess got the gold apple; but when the girl came up to the Prince's bedroom at night he was fast asleep. She called him and shook him, and between whiles she wept sore; but for all she could do she couldn't wake him up. Next morning as soon as day broke, came the Princess with the long nose, and drove her out again.

So in the daytime she sat down under the castle windows and began to card with her golden carding comb, and the same thing happened. The Princess asked what she wanted for it, and she said it wasn't for sale for gold or money, but if she might get leave to go up to the Prince and be with him that night, the Princess should have it. But when she went up she found him fast asleep again, and all she called, and she shook him, and wept, and prayed, she couldn't get life into him; and as soon as the first gray peep of day came, then came the Princess with the long nose and chased her out again.

So, in the daytime the girl sat down outside under the castle window, and began to spin with her golden spinning wheel, and that, too, the Princess with the long nose wanted to have. So she threw up the window and asked what she wanted for it. The girl said, as she had said twice before, it wasn't for sale for gold or money; but if she might go up to the Prince who was there, and be with him alone that night, she might have it.

Yes, she might do that and welcome. But now you must know there were some Christian folk who had been carried off thither, and as they sat in their room, which was next the Prince, they had heard

how a woman had been in there, and wept and prayed, and called to
him two nights running, and they told that to the Prince.

That evening, when the Princess came with her sleepy drink,
the Prince made as if he drank, but threw it over his shoulder, for
he could guess it was a sleepy drink. So, when the girl came in, she
found the Prince wide awake; and then she told him the whole story
how she had come thither.

"Ah," said the Prince, "you've just come in the very nick of time,
for tomorrow is to be our wedding day; but now I won't have the
Long-nose, and you are the only woman in the world who can set
me free. I'll say I want to see what my wife is fit for, and beg her to
wash the shirt which has the three spots of tallow on it; she'll say
yes, for she doesn't know 'tis you who put them there; but that's
work only for Christian folk, and not for such a pack of trolls, and so
I'll say that I won't have any other for my bride than the woman who
can wash them out, and then I'll ask you to do it."

So there was great joy and love between them all that night. The
next day, when the wedding was to be, the Prince said,

"First of all, I'd like to see what my bride is fit for."

"Yes!" said the stepmother, with all her heart.

"Well," said the Prince, "I've got a fine shirt which I'd like for
my wedding shirt, but somehow or other it has got three spots of
tallow on it, which I must have washed out; and I have sworn never
to take any other bride than the woman who's able to do that. If she
can't, she's not worth having."

Well, that was no great thing they said, so they agreed, and she
with the long nose began to wash away as hard as she could, but the
more she rubbed and scrubbed, the bigger the spots grew.

"Ah!" said the old hag, her mother, "you can't wash; let me try."

But she hadn't long taken the shirt in hand, before it got far
worse than ever, and with all her rubbing, and wringing, and

scrubbing, the spots grew bigger and blacker, and darker and uglier was the shirt.

Then all the other trolls began to wash, but the longer it lasted, the blacker and uglier the shirt grew, till at last it was as black all over as if it had been up the chimney.

"Ah!" said the Prince, "you're none of you worth a straw; you can't wash. Why, there, outside, sits a beggar lassie; I'll be bound she knows how to wash better than the whole lot of you. COME IN LASSIE!" he shouted.

Well, in she came.

"Can you wash this shirt clean, lassie, you?" said he.

"I don't know," she said, "but I can try."

And almost before she had taken it and dipped it in the water, it was as white as driven snow, and whiter still.

"Yes; you are the girl for me," said the Prince.

At that the old hag flew into such a rage, she burst on the spot, and the Princess with the long nose, after her, and the whole pack of trolls after her—at least I've never heard a word about them since.

As for the Prince and the Princess, they set free all the poor Christian folk who had been carried off and shut up there; and they took with them all the silver and gold, and flitted away as far as they could from the castle that lay East O' The Sun And West O' The Moon.

THE REWARD
OF THE WORLD

* ** ** *

ONCE upon a time there was a man who went out in the woods to cut some rafters. But he could not find the kind of trees he needed— long, slim and straight, until he came high upon the mountainside, beneath a great scree. There he heard cries and wailing, as if somebody was in the throes of death. He went up to see, what this might be, whether somebody needed help. Then he heard, the cries came from underneath a large flat stone in the scree—it was so heavy, it would take several men to lift it. But the man went down into the wood, cut a sapling which he made into a lever, and with the lever he got the big flat stone weighed up somewhat.

From under the stone came a dragon, and it wanted to eat the man. "Now really," said the man, "here I've just saved your life, and now you want to eat me for my pains; this is uncommonly ungrateful."

"Maybe," the dragon said, "but you can imagine, I am starving, I have been lying here for one hundred years and never tasted a morsel of meat. And such is the reward of the world."

The man pleaded and begged for his life, and at last they agreed, that the first passer-by they would take for an umpire. If he judged otherwise, the man was not to lose his life, but if he agreed with the dragon, the dragon might eat the man.

The first passer-by was an old dog, whom they spied on the road that ran by the foot of the hillside. They called to him and asked him to come and judge between them.

"God knows, I have served my master faithfully ever since I was a puppy," the dog said. "Many a night I have watched, whilst he snored in his bed. I have saved his house and home from fire and thieves' hands more than once. But now I am deaf and blind, and now he wants to shoot me, so I had to run away and stray from place to place, begging my food until I shall die of hunger. No, such is the reward of the world."

"Then, I'll eat you," the dragon said, and prepared to gobble up the man.

But the man pleaded his cause very well, and he begged for his life so fervently, so in the end they agreed to take for umpire the next body who came along. If he said the same thing as the dog and the dragon, the dragon might eat the man and get a meal of human flesh. But if he did not agree, the man was to get away alive.

Then an old horse came hobbling along, on the road beneath the hillside. They spoke to him and asked him to pass judgment in their dispute. Well, the horse was willing.

"Now I have served my master as long as I was able to draw or carry," said the horse. "I have toiled and slaved for him, until the sweat ran from every hair of my body, and I have labored faithfully, until my joints stiffened, and I am worn out with hard work and old age. Now I am of no use to him, he says, I am not worth my feed, and now he is going to give me a bullet, he says. No, such is the reward of the world."

But again the man begged fervently for his life.

But the dragon said, he wanted a mouthful of human flesh, he was so hungry he could not contain himself any longer.

"Look who is coming, as if he was sent to be our judge," said the man. Mikkel the fox came sauntering towards them from among the stones in the scree. "All good things come by threes," the man said. "Let me ask him too, and if he decides the same as the others did, you may eat me at once."

"Very well then," said the dragon, for he too had heard, that all good things come by threes. So he was willing to let it go at that.

The man talked to the fox, the same as he had to the other two. "Well, well," said the fox, but then he pulled the man a little to one side.

"What would be my fee, if I save you from the dragon?" the fox whispered in his ear.

"You may come to my place every Thursday night and be the master of my chickens and my geese," said the man.

"We'll have to investigate on the site of the alleged happenings, my dear dragon," said the fox. "I cannot picture in my mind, how you, who are such a large and powerful creature, could ever find room to lie down beneath that slab of stone."

"Oh, but I was lying here on this hillside, sunning myself, when an avalanche of stone came and buried me beneath the slab."

"Possibly," said Mikkel, "yet I cannot see it, and I won't believe it, until I have seen it."

Then they had better make a test, the man proposed, and the dragon slipped down in the hole. Quickly the man snatched away the lever, and the slab of stone clapped down upon the dragon.

"Now lie there until doomsday," said the fox. "Or wouldn't you eat the man who had saved your life, or how is it?" The dragon cried and wailed, but the two others went away.

The first Thursday night the fox decided, he would visit the hencoop to be master there. He hid behind a stack of cordwood, and when the maid came in the evening to feed the chickens, Mikkel slipped in. She did not notice, and did not see him, and she had scarcely left, before he started. He killed chickens, enough to feed upon for a week, and then he gorged himself until he was hardly able to stir. When she returned next morning, there was the fox, sleeping and snoring in the morning sun, with all four legs sprawling, and he had stuffed himself as full and as round as a sausage.

The maid hurried up to the house and called the goodwife, and she and all her maids arrived with sticks and poles, and they went for Mikkel, beating him almost to death. But just as he was nearly done for, and the women were sure he was about to give up his ghost, he discovered a hole in the floor. He got through, and limped and dragged himself home to the woods. "Wau, wau, such is the reward of the world, and that's the truth," said Mikkel the fox.

Designed by Fiona Cecile Clarke, the Cluny Media *logo
depicts a monk at work in the scriptorium,
with a cat sitting at his feet.*

*The monk represents our mission to emulate
the invaluable contributions of the monks
of Cluny in preserving the libraries of the West,
our strivings to know and love the truth.*

*The cat at the monk's feet is Pangur Bán, from the
eponymous Irish poem of the 9th century.
The anonymous poet compares his scholarly
pursuit of truth with the cat's happy hunting of mice.
The depiction of Pangur Bán is an homage to the work
of the monks of Irish monasteries and a sign
of the joy we at Cluny take in our trade.*

"Messe ocus Pangur Bán,
cechtar nathar fria saindan:
bíth a menmasam fri seilgg,
mu memna céin im saincheirdd."

Made in the USA
Middletown, DE
28 April 2023

29490706R00136